S0-BRB-800

INTRODUCING
ISSUES
WITH

OPPOSING VIEWPOINTS®

AIDS

Other books in the Introducing Issues
with Opposing Viewpoints series:

INTRODUCING
ISSUES
WITH

OPPOSING VIEWPOINTS®

AIDS

Andrea C. Nakaya, *Book Editor*

Bruce Glassman, *Vice President*
Bonnie Szumski, *Publisher, Series Editor*
Helen Cothran, *Managing Editor*

OPPOSING
VIEWPOINTS®
SERIES

GREENHAVEN PRESS
An imprint of Thomson Gale, a part of The Thomson Corporation

THOMSON
GALE

Detroit • New York • San Francisco • San Diego • New Haven, Conn. • Waterville, Maine • London • Munich

For more information, contact
Greenhaven Press
27500 Drake Rd.
Farmington Hills, MI 48331-3535
Or you can visit our Internet site at http://www.gale.com

LIBRARY OF CONGRESS CATALOGING-IN-PUBLICATION DATA

AIDS / Andrea C. Nakaya, book editor.
     p. cm. — (Introducing issues with opposing viewpoints)
   Includes bibliographical references and index.
   ISBN 0-7377-3218-0 (lib. bdg. : alk. paper)
   1. AIDS (Disease)—Epidemiology. 2. AIDS (Disease)—Government policy. 3. AIDS (Disease)—Africa. I. Nakaya, Andrea C., 1976– . II. Series.
   RA643.8.A37 2006
   614.5'99392'0096—dc22

                                                                    2005047417

Printed in the United States of America

CONTENTS

Chapter 3: How Should AIDS in Africa Be Addressed?

Indulging in a wide spectrum of ideas, beliefs, and perspectives is a critical cornerstone of democracy. After all, it is often debates over differences of opinion, such as whether to legalize abortion, how to treat prisoners, or when to enact the death penalty that shape our society and drive it forward. Such diversity of thought is frequently regarded as the hallmark of a healthy and civilized culture. As the Reverend Clifford Schutjer of the First Congregational Church in Mansfield, Ohio, declared in a 2001 sermon, "Surrounding oneself with only like-minded people, restricting what we listen to or read only to what we find agreeable is irresponsible. Refusing to entertain doubts once we make up our minds is a subtle but deadly form of arrogance." With this advice in mind, Introducing Issues with Opposing Viewpoints books aim to open readers' minds to the critically divergent views that comprise our world's most important debates.

Introducing Issues with Opposing Viewpoints simplifies for students the enormous and often overwhelming mass of material now available via print and electronic media. Collected in every volume is an array of opinions that capture the essence of a particular controversy or topic. Introducing Issues with Opposing Viewpoints books embody the spirit of nineteenth-century journalist Charles A. Dana's axiom: "Fight for your opinions, but do not believe that they contain the whole truth, or the only truth." Absorbing such contrasting opinions teaches students to analyze the strength of an argument and compare it to its opposition. From this process readers can inform and strengthen their own opinions, or be exposed to new information that will change their minds. Introducing Issues with Opposing Viewpoints is a mosaic of different voices. The authors are statesmen, pundits, academics, journalists, corporations, and ordinary people who have felt compelled to share their experiences and ideas in a public forum. Their words have been collected from newspapers, journals, books, speeches, interviews, and the Internet, the fastest growing body of opinionated material in the world.

Introducing Issues with Opposing Viewpoints shares many of the well-known features of its critically acclaimed parent series, Opposing Viewpoints. The articles are presented in a pro/con format, allowing readers to absorb divergent perspectives side by side. Active reading questions preface each viewpoint, requiring the student to approach the material thoughtfully and carefully. Useful charts, graphs, and cartoons supplement each article. A thorough introduction provides readers with crucial background on an issue. An annotated bibliography points the reader toward articles, books, and Web sites that contain additional information on the topic. An appendix of organizations to contact contains a wide variety of charities, nonprofit organizations, political groups, and private enterprises that each hold a position on the issue at hand. Finally, a comprehensive index allows readers to locate content quickly and efficiently.

Introducing Issues with Opposing Viewpoints is also significantly different from Opposing Viewpoints. As the series title implies, its presentation will help introduce students to the concept of opposing viewpoints, and learn to use this material to aid in critical writing and debate. The series' four-color, accessible format makes the books attractive and inviting to readers of all levels. In addition, each viewpoint has been carefully edited to maximize a reader's understanding of the content. Short but thorough viewpoints capture the essence of an argument. A substantial, thought-provoking essay question placed at the end of each viewpoint asks the student to further investigate the issues raised in the viewpoint, compare and contrast two authors' arguments, or consider how one might go about forming an opinion on the topic at hand. Each viewpoint contains sidebars that include at-a-glance information and handy statistics. A Facts About section located in the back of the book further supplies students with relevant facts and figures.

Following in the tradition of the Opposing Viewpoints series, Greenhaven Press continues to provide readers with invaluable exposure to the controversial issues that shape our world. As John Stuart Mill once wrote: "The only way in which a human being can make some approach to knowing the whole of a subject is by hearing what can be said about it by persons of every variety of opinion and studying all modes in which it can be looked at by every character of mind. No wise man ever acquired his wisdom in any mode but this." It is to this principle that Introducing Issues with Opposing Viewpoints books are dedicated.

INTRODUCTION

"Since the advent of [AIDS drugs], the disease has been transformed into a treatable and chronic condition for a significant proportion of those with access to this treatment. Yet 95% of the . . . HIV-infected individuals in the world live in low-income countries, and only a tiny fraction of these people have access to [these drugs]."

—members of the faculty of Harvard University

In 1991 U.S. basketball star Magic Johnson shocked the nation by announcing that he had contracted HIV, the virus that causes AIDS. At that time, diagnosis with HIV meant that a person was likely to die from AIDS within a few years, and most people believed that Johnson would be no exception; however, he proved them wrong. Johnson continued to both play and coach basketball, founded the

In 1991 basketball superstar Magic Johnson (center) shocked the nation with his announcement that he was HIV-positive.

Magic Johnson Foundation to fight AIDS, and became a successful businessman. In 2005, fourteen years after his diagnosis, Johnson is alive and healthy. "Most people . . . can't even live my life," he says. "Trust me. I get up at 5:30–6 every morning. I'm in the gym. I run a couple miles. I lift weights, and then I'm at work until 8–9 o'clock at night." According to him, "The only time I think about HIV is when I have to take my medicine twice a day." Johnson's story is an example of how antiretroviral drugs have radically altered the meaning of an HIV or AIDS diagnosis. These drugs delay the onset of AIDS, dramatically reduce its symptoms, and greatly extend life. This accomplishment, however, has generated both praise and criticism.

Some people applaud the development of antiretroviral medications. While there is still no cure for HIV, these drugs are highly successful at

This Kenyan woman and her child are both HIV-positive. An estimated 2.4 million people in sub-Saharan Africa have HIV or AIDS.

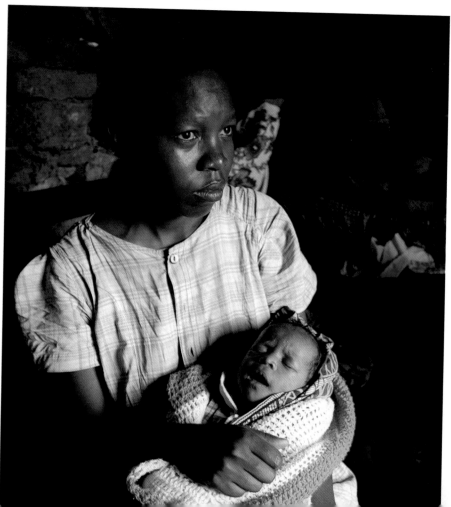

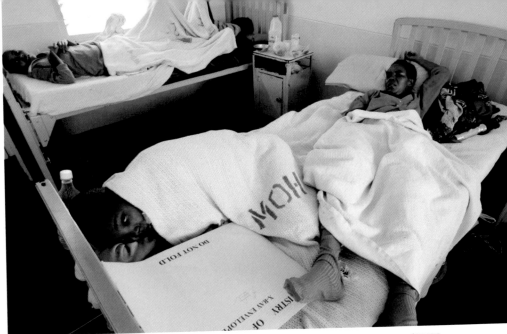

Women with AIDS await treatment in a Kenyan hospital. Less than 2 percent of HIV-positive people in sub-Saharan Africa receive proper treatment.

preventing illness and a slow death from the disease. Michael Hickson, senior vice president and chief medical officer of Housing Works in New York City, believes that HIV patients on antiretroviral medication could theoretically live about the same amount of time as people who are not infected. "I know patients who are 15 years out on therapy and who are still fine," he says. Michael Shernoff, a psychotherapist in New York City has worked with HIV-infected patients since the 1980s. He echoes Hickson's observations. "I had 150 deaths in the first 15 years of the epidemic," says Shernoff, "but have not had anyone be seriously ill from HIV or from AIDS and no deaths in the last 10 years."

However, critics point out that for the majority of people with HIV or AIDS, the development of antiretroviral drugs is meaningless, because they do not have access to them. For example, an estimated 2.4 million people in sub-Saharan Africa have HIV or AIDS, yet less than 2 percent receive AIDS drugs. Stephen Lewis, the United Nations special envoy for HIV/AIDS in Africa, describes how this has impacted that country. He explains that without these lifesaving drugs, Africans "are now dying in astronomical numbers." To illustrate the extent of the problem, he describes a trip to Africa: "You visit almost any of the hospitals in Southern Africa . . . and there are two and three patients to a bed. And under every bed and on the concrete floor lies another patient. . . . Eighty to 90 per cent, sometimes 95 per cent of the cases in the hospitals are now related to AIDS." Africa is not the only place in need of antiretrovirals. The reality is that most of these drugs go to a small number of people in wealthy nations, leaving the majority of those with HIV or AIDS to die from the disease. According to a 2004 report by the United Nations, just 7 percent of people in developing countries who need the drugs have access to them.

Advocates of antiretroviral drugs maintain that this situation is changing. As the drugs become cheaper and easier to manufacture, they will become more widely available in less-wealthy countries such as Africa, it is argued. Recent, dramatic price decreases for antiretroviral medicines support the argument. According to journalist Geoffrey Cowley, the cost of the drugs has fallen by as much as 98 percent in recent years. This means that the life of someone with HIV or AIDS can be saved for less than $1 a day, says Cowley. Some proponents cite the case of Brazil, a country with limited financial resources, to prove that AIDS drugs are beginning to make their way to the less fortunate. Brazil has delivered free antiretroviral drugs to virtually every AIDS patient in need. From 1996 to 2002, the country saw a 40 to 70 percent decrease in mortality rates and a sevenfold drop in hospitalization needs.

Yet some people charge that the effectiveness of antiretroviral drugs in treating HIV and AIDS is actually decreasing the likelihood that people in developing nations will receive them. They believe that because people in wealthy countries are not dying from AIDS, they forget it is still a deadly disease. Thus, there is less effort to get cheap drugs to the people in those countries where HIV and AIDS are still destroying populations. Journalist Nick Schulz explains: "HIV infection—while still terrible—has been transformed into a chronic, manageable condition." He says, "It will fall from the developed world's radar screen while it devastates the impoverished corners of the globe."

As the heated debate over antiretroviral drugs illustrates, AIDS is an important issue that is having a serious impact on citizens of every nation. The authors in *Introducing Issues with Opposing Viewpoints: AIDS* explore other facets of this controversial topic. While there remain a multitude of opinions and a definite lack of consensus on these issues, the answers are vitally important as AIDS remains an incurable disease that continues to kill millions of people around the world every year.

CHAPTER 1

Is the Global AIDS Epidemic Exaggerated?

An emaciated Kenyan man infected with HIV stares disconsolately at the ground.

VIEWPOINT 1

The AIDS Epidemic Is a Global Threat

Edward Susman

"The AIDS epidemic has become a mounting global tragedy."

In the following viewpoint Edward Susman warns that AIDS is a serious problem that is devastating populations around the world. The epidemic is most severe in Africa, explains Susman, however, it is also spreading rapidly through Asia, the Caribbean, Latin America, and eastern Europe, where it is dramatically altering life expectancies and economic development. While western Europe and the United States have been more successful in controlling the epidemic, he says, AIDS is still a threat in these countries too. Susman is a freelance writer and a regular contributor to United Press International, a leading news provider.

AS YOU READ, CONSIDER THE FOLLOWING QUESTIONS:

1. In the author's opinion, what factors have caused the AIDS epidemic in Africa to continue?
2. In how many Caribbean and Latin American countries are HIV infection rates higher than 1 percent, according to Susman?
3. Among which group in the United States have HIV diagnoses increased, according to the author?

The AIDS epidemic has become a mounting global tragedy, with 20 million killed and 40 million infected. Worldwide in 2003, according to estimates from the Joint United Nations Programme on HIV/AIDS (UNAIDS), roughly five million people were infected with HIV. More than three million are expected to die from complications of the disease in 2004.

Africa

In Africa, the pandemic's effects are unmatched in their severity and tragic consequences. About 29.4 million of those infected with or dying of HIV/AIDS live in sub-Saharan Africa, where the virus spread to 3.2 million more people in 2003 alone and 58 percent of those living with HIV are women. Although the horror and extent of the disease on the African continent have brought promises of assistance from world leaders, including President George W. Bush, a combination of poverty, government inaction, myth, and stigma continues to drive the epidemic to levels that are difficult for citizens of the developed countries to comprehend. . . .

In Africa, where 16 nations have disease prevalence rates that exceed 10 percent—20 times the 0.5 percent HIV incidence rate in the United States and western Europe—many governments have ignored the epidemic that fills hospital wards and leaves millions of homeless orphans in its wake. . . .

Asia

While Africa's social, economic, and humanitarian catastrophe has caught the world's attention, a pending AIDS disaster in Asia barely causes a blip on the radar screen.

Officials are aware of the disease's growing incidence in India and China, which are home to more than 2 billion people. They have sounded alarms, but in vulnerable, undereducated, and poverty-stricken areas, those warnings may go unheard.

Consider India. Officially, just under 4 million people are living with HIV infection in the world's most populous democracy, but many doctors in the field think this figure is underestimated.

UNAIDS reports some progress: "New behavioral studies in India suggest that prevention efforts directed at specific populations such

Estimated Number of Adults and Children Living with AIDS

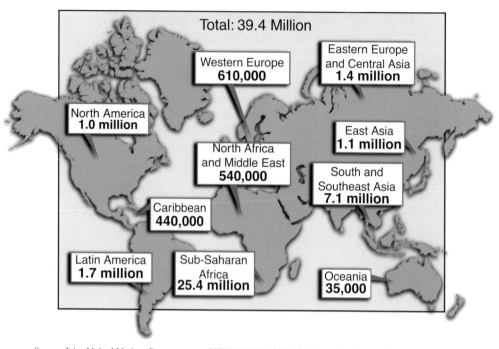

Source: Joint United Nations Programme on HIV/AIDS/World Health Organization, 2004.

as female sex workers and injecting drug users are paying dividends in some states, in the form of higher HIV/AIDS knowledge and condom use.

"However," it reports, "HIV prevalence among those key groups continues to increase in some states, underlining the need for well-planned and sustained interventions on a large scale." . . .

The Caribbean and Latin America

Although AIDS was recognized and identified in the United States and Europe in the 1980s, the extent of the disease throughout the Caribbean and Latin America is still underappreciated. According to UNAIDS: "In several Caribbean countries, adult HIV prevalence rates are surpassed only by the rates experienced in sub-Saharan Africa—making this the second-most affected region in the world."

"I don't think that the situation in Latin America and the Caribbean will ever come close to Africa, where infection rates among adults exceed 10, 15, or 20 percent. But there are already a number of countries in Latin America that have infection rates that exceed 1 percent—and that really is troublesome," said Dr. Richard Keenlyside of the Centers for Disease Control and Prevention [CDC] in Atlanta.

Reports show that the HIV infection rate is higher than 1 percent in 12 countries in the region. This might not seem very high, but at that level the disease already affects overall life expectancy and economic development.

Among the nations that have prevalence rates above 1 percent are impoverished Haiti at 6 percent and the Bahamas at 3.5 percent. Throughout the region, 1.9 million people—nearly half a million in the Caribbean—are infected with HIV. . . .

Eastern Europe
As knowledge of how to control the AIDS epidemic improves, hopes are raised that its spread will be checked. Eastern Europe is one place where those hopes are illusory, as there is a great chasm between knowledge and the political will to act.

A young HIV-positive boy eats a bowl of soup in a Moscow hospital. Throughout eastern Europe, approximately 1.2 million people are infected with HIV.

Dr. Scott Hammer, professor of infectious diseases at Columbia University, bit his lip and thought about how to describe the AIDS epidemic in eastern Europe. "Explosive," he said. "Explosive."

In countries such as Belarus, Ukraine, Russia, and Uzbekistan, the epidemic is roaring through populations of injecting drug users and is evident among people with other sexually transmitted diseases. In the region, 1.2 million people are infected with HIV.

The 28 states that make up eastern Europe are strapped for cash to run prevention campaigns and treatment programs. More tragically, the governments of the region have generally avoided learning anything from the mistakes made in the West and Africa, where the epidemic is more mature. Dr. Peter Piot, executive director of UNAIDS, singled out Russia for specific criticism, saying the nation expends few resources in fighting the epidemic and does not even have a high-ranking official in charge of those meager efforts. . . .

Western Europe

While the situation in eastern Europe is worrisome, the wealthier states of western Europe have their own problems with the epidemic. Up to 10 percent of people infected with HIV have a mutated virus that is resistant to at least one class of drugs used to treat the disease.

FAST FACT

Women comprise an increasing proportion of the total number of adults living with HIV or AIDS, rising from 41 percent in 1997 to 47 percent in 2004.

"Transmission of resistant virus occurs," said Dr. David van de Vijver, an epidemiologist at the University Medical Center in Utrecht, the Netherlands. The pan-European survey looked at rates of drug-resistant virus from 17 countries. In western Europe, an estimated 570,000 people are living with HIV/AIDS.

While most of those countries have stable rates of overall infection, there are still pockets of alarming increases in new infection rates, notably in cities in Portugal and Italy. "We were used to thinking that the epidemic in western Europe was stable," said Lucas Wiessing, a researcher with the European Monitoring Centre for Drugs and Drug Addiction in Lisbon. "But we have found that despite

Source: Parker. © 2002 by Cagle Cartoons, Inc. Reproduced by permission.

prevention measures, HIV transmission continues at high rates among subgroups of injecting drug users in some countries."

"The situation in Portugal is very scary," said van de Vijver.

The United States

Even in the United States, government agencies are expressing concerns that the "stable" epidemic is showing signs of instability. In this country, 900,000 people are infected with HIV; 180,000 of these are women, 10,000 are children under the age of 15, and there are hints that infection rates are on the rise again. According to Dr. Harold Jaffe, director of the CDC's National Center for HIV, Sexually Transmitted Disease, and Tuberculosis, an increasing number of new HIV infections are being diagnosed among gay and bisexual men. From 2001 to 2002, the number of new HIV diagnoses per year rose 7.1 percent among that population; in the three years from 1999 to 2002, the number of new HIV diagnoses per year has increased by 17.7 percent.

"The AIDS epidemic in the United States is far from over," said Jaffe. "While effective treatments are crucial in our fight against HIV, preventing infection in the first place is still the only true protection against the serious and fatal consequences of this disease."

A World at Risk

Undoubtedly, a few rays of sunshine may pierce the darkness of the HIV/AIDS pandemic, especially in the wealthier nations. For the majority of the 40 million people now infected, however—and the millions more who will become infected with the killer disease this year [2004] and next—the sunshine eludes them. Instead, the shadow of a disease that robs people of their most productive years and extends over families, communities, and nations spreads relentlessly across the landscape.

EVALUATING THE AUTHORS' ARGUMENTS:

In the viewpoint you just read, Edward Susman warns that the AIDS epidemic is escalating. In the next viewpoint, Michael Fumento contends that warnings about AIDS are vastly exaggerated. In your opinion, which of the two authors makes the most persuasive argument? Explain.

The AIDS Epidemic Is Exaggerated

Michael Fumento

"Even the most honest AIDS researchers are tempted to exaggerate because everyone else does."

The extent of the global AIDS epidemic has been vastly exaggerated, argues Michael Fumento in the following viewpoint. Because it is impossible to individually count the number of people with AIDS worldwide, numbers are extrapolated from smaller surveys, he explains, and require estimation. Fumento argues that researchers, encouraged by the United Nations, incorrectly estimate high in order to receive funding for AIDS research and prevention. According to him, this overestimation is harmful because it results in misallocation of funds between AIDS and other diseases. Fumento is a senior fellow with the Hudson Institute in Washington, D.C., and author of numerous books, including *The Myth of Heterosexual AIDS*.

AS YOU READ, CONSIDER THE FOLLOWING QUESTIONS:

1. In opposition to dire predictions about AIDS deaths in Africa, what has actually happened to the population there, as argued by Fumento?

2. According to the 2004 *Boston Globe* report cited by the author, by how much may the number of global AIDS infections have been pumped up?
3. How does Fumento answer the argument that the billions of dollars spent fighting terrorism in Iraq could have eradicated AIDS?

"At least 30 percent of the entire adult population of Central Africa is infected with the AIDS virus," a doctor tells a U.S. newspaper. A high Ugandan official says that within two years his nation will "be a desert." ABC [American Broadcasting Company] News *Nightline* declares that within 12 years "50 million Africans may have died of AIDS."

Actually, those statements and predictions were all made between 1986 and 1988. Yet since 1985, Central Africa's population has increased over 70 percent while Uganda's has nearly doubled. Japan, conversely, has close to no AIDS cases yet its population growth has essentially stopped.

According to the UN's [United Nations'] latest estimate, *Nightline* predicted 50 million dead Africans by the year 2000 was actually 20 million dead worldwide by the end of [2003].

Crying "Wolf" About AIDS

AIDS is a horrible disease. But let's be sensible about the scope of the problem. I've been writing about the exaggeration of the AIDS epidemic since 1987, so I know when the crying of "Wolf!" will stop. Never. Indeed, at the just-concluded 15th annual UN AIDS conference in Bangkok [in July 2004] the will o' the wisp wolves again were everywhere and the media questioned nothing.

For example, there was Peter Piot, executive director of the UN AIDS program, bemoaning that "Projections NOW suggest that some countries in sub-Saharan Africa will face *economic collapse* unless they bring their epidemics under control." (Emphasis added.) He should know; he's been using those exact words for at least five years.

Nor is there any reason to accept that 20-million-dead figure, nor that almost five million new people became infected last year [in 2003] or that almost three million died of AIDS.

Higher Numbers Mean More Money

The epidemic always has and always will refuse to live up to the official predictions for one simple reason: The louder the Klaxon sounds, the more public and private contributions pour in. The UN AIDS program doesn't even care if it contradicts other UN branches—where do you think I got those population increase numbers?

Peter Piot, executive director of the UN AIDS program, has been accused of exaggerating the scope of the world's AIDS problem.

The *Boston Globe* reported in June [2004] that two U.S. AIDS officials, speaking on condition of anonymity, said they think global HIV numbers may be pumped up by 50 percent. [University of California at] Berkeley epidemiologist Dr. James Chin puts the inflation range at 25 percent to 40 percent.

Chin became responsible for California's AIDS surveillance program when the disease was detected in 1981. In 1987, he became chief of the UN's Surveillance, Forecasting, and Impact Assessment unit of the Global Program on AIDS, where he quickly saw the agency was using an estimated range of worldwide cases that was far too high. Ultimately, the UN agreed with Chin's assessment and he stayed on another five years.

In the beginning, he says, some countries would understate their figures for fear of becoming pariahs and losing tourism. "But the pendulum swung so that it was in vogue to claim high numbers" in order to get more attention and more money.

Despite the effect of AIDS, Uganda's population has nearly doubled over the last twenty years.

The problem is that AIDS and HIV victims don't walk through turnstiles to be counted. People conduct surveys and then somebody extrapolates from them. That's where the hanky-panky occurs.

"They don't falsify per se," Chin told me, but "as an epidemiologist I look at these numbers and how they're derived. Every step of the way there is a range and you can choose the low end or the high end. Almost consistently the high end was chosen."

The *Globe* reported that "Several years ago, UNAIDS estimated that up to 60 percent of the Angolan military was HIV positive," but the head of the US Department of Defense's HIV/AIDS Prevention Program told the paper that the figure was "nowhere near close to that. It's 6 to 7 percent. They based the earlier number on a small sample, which included people outside the military, and extrapolated that to the military as a whole."

As extrapolations go from a carefully chosen area, namely those known to have high infection rates, to an entire country the overestimates just keep multiplying. That's just what the UN wants. "There are those who believe the UN line, and they see me as Public Enemy Number One," he says. "And then there are those who know what's going on and keep up the charade because they don't want to lose the money and attention."

Exaggeration Harms Prevention Efforts

"What they don't seem to realize," he says, "is that this causes serious misallocations between AIDS and other diseases and even between the needs of AIDS programs in different countries."

As such, even the most honest AIDS researchers are tempted to exaggerate because everyone else does. An AIDS health official in a southern African country whom I've known for 15 years told me he found this out the hard [way] when approached with potential funding by one of the largest private AIDS donors, the Henry J. Kaiser Family Foundation. But first, they wanted a survey of the problem. Rather than bloating the figures, he blew it and told the truth. Kaiser huffed and took its funds elsewhere.

In 2004 UN secretary general Kofi Annan accused the United States of treating the AIDS epidemic with less regard than the threat of terrorism.

Is this any way to combat an epidemic?

Naturally, as with everything else, global AIDS is all America's fault. Never mind that with less than a third of the world's GDP [gross domestic product], the U.S. government is spending twice as much on the problem this year [2004] as the rest of the planet combined. UN Secretary-General Kofi Annan ripped the U.S. for not taking AIDS as serious as worldwide terrorism. Activists like actor Richard

Gere, associated with the Kaiser Foundation, insist that "The $200–300 billion spent in Iraq probably could have eradicated this illness," as if you can just put money into one slot of a machine and watch a cure drop out of another.

Still, while AIDS may be grossly exaggerated and Richard Gere utterly obnoxious, it is a terrible disease affecting all countries. That's why we must know precisely where to spend our money. Unfortunately, neither the UN nor its staunch media allies are about to tell us.

EVALUATING THE AUTHOR'S ARGUMENTS:

Michael Fumento uses both quotes from experts and statistics to help support his contention that the AIDS epidemic has been exaggerated. Which of these do you believe best helps increase the effectiveness of his argument? Why?

AIDS Is a Serious Problem in Africa

AIDS Alert International

"AIDS has become a full-blown development crisis [in Africa]."

AIDS Alert International is an organization that works to prevent the spread of AIDS, through community-based research, publications, workshops, conferences, and support programs. In the following viewpoint the organization asserts that AIDS has become a serious problem in Africa. Because the nation failed to take early action to curtail the spread of the disease, it has spread rapidly across the continent, states AIDS Alert, and now infects a large percentage of the population. According to the organization, AIDS is killing large numbers of Africans, creating millions of orphans, and destroying the continent's economic and social structure. Africa and the international community must take action to stop the ravages of this disease, maintains AIDS Alert.

AS YOU READ, CONSIDER THE FOLLOWING QUESTIONS:

1. According to the author, of the 2001 global total of 3 million AIDS deaths, how many occurred in Africa?
2. How has AIDS affected the supply of teachers in Africa, as explained by AIDS Alert International?
3. How many billions of dollars a year are needed to begin successfully fighting AIDS in Africa, according to the author?

AIDS Alert International, "HIV & AIDS in Africa," www.aidsalert.org.uk, 2004. Copyright © 2004 by AIDS Alert International. All rights reserved. Reproduced by permission.

Africa continues to dwarf the rest of the world in how the region has been affected by AIDS. Africa is home to 70% of the adults and 80% of the children living with HIV in the world. The estimated number of newly infected adults and children in Africa reached 3.5 million at the end of 2001. It has also been estimated that 28.5 million adults and children were living with HIV/AIDS in Africa by the end of the year. AIDS deaths totalled 3 million globally in 2001, and of the global total 2.2 million AIDS deaths occurred in Africa.

In sub-Saharan Africa HIV is now deadlier than war itself. In 1998, 200,000 Africans died in war, but more than 2 million died of AIDS. AIDS has become a full-blown development crisis. Its social and economic consequences are felt widely not only in health but in education, industry, agriculture, transport, human resources and the economy in general. . . .

How Are Different Countries Affected?

National HIV prevalence rates vary widely between countries. They range from under 2% of the adult population in some West African countries to around 20% or more in the southern part of the continent, with countries in Central and East Africa having rates midway

Surrounded by family, a Zambian woman mourns the loss of her daughter to AIDS. The vast majority of the world's HIV-positive population lives in African nations.

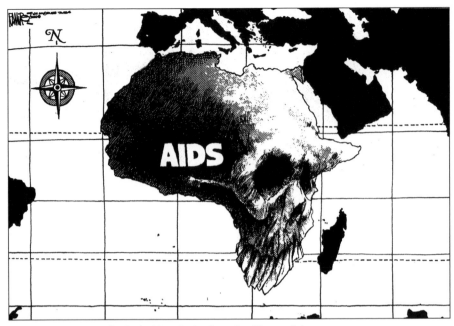

Source: Ramirez. © 2000 by Copley News Service. Reproduced by permission.

between these. However, prevalence rates do not convey people's life-time risk of becoming infected and dying of AIDS. In the eight African countries where at least 15% of today's adults are infected, conservative analyses show that AIDS will claim the lives of around a third of today's 15 year olds.

Sixteen African countries south of the Sahara have more than one-tenth of the adult population aged 15–49 infected with HIV. In seven countries, all in the southern cone of the continent, at least one adult in five is living with the virus.

- In Botswana a shocking 38.8 % of adults are now infected with HIV
- In South Africa 20.1% of adults are infected with HIV. With a total of 5 million infected people, South Africa has the largest number of people living with HIV/AIDS in the world.

West Africa is relatively less affected by HIV infection, but the prevalence rates in some large countries are creeping up.

- Côte d'Ivoire is already among the 15 worst affected countries in the world.

- Nigeria, by far the most populous country in sub-Saharan Africa, has 5.8% of its adult population infected with HIV.

Infection rates in East Africa, once the highest on the continent, hover above those in the West of the continent but have been exceeded by the rates now being seen in the Southern cone.

- The prevalence rate among adults in Kenya has reached double-digit figures and continues to rise. In Kenya 15% of the adult population (15–49) are living with HIV/AIDS.

What Is the Result of This?

Over and above the personal suffering that accompanies HIV infection wherever it strikes, the virus in sub-Saharan Africa threatens to devastate whole communities, rolling back decades of progress towards a healthier and more prosperous future.

Sub-Saharan Africa faces a triple challenge of colossal proportions:

- bringing health care, support and solidarity to a growing population of people with HIV-related illness,
- reducing the annual toll of new infections by enabling individuals to protect themselves and others,
- coping with the cumulative impact of over 17 million AIDS deaths on orphans and other survivors, on communities, and on national development.

> **FAST FACT**
>
> According to the Joint United Nations Programme on HIV/AIDS, an estimated 12 million children living in sub-Saharan Africa have been orphaned due to AIDS.

Millions of adults are dying young or in early middle age. They leave behind children grieving and struggling to survive without a parent's care. Many of those dying have surviving partners who are themselves infected and in need of care. Their families have to find money to pay for their funerals, and employers, schools, factories and hospitals have to train other staff to replace them at the workplace. . . .

Education

The effect on education is that AIDS now threatens the coverage and quality of education. The epidemic has not spared this sector any more than it has spared health, agriculture or mining.

On the demand side, HIV is reducing the numbers of children in school. HIV positive women have fewer babies, in part because they may die before the end of their childbearing years, and up to a third of their children are themselves infected and may not survive until school age. Also, many children have lost their parents to AIDS, or are living in households which have taken in AIDS orphans, and they may be forced to drop out of school to start earning money, or simply because school fees have become unaffordable.

On the supply side, teacher shortages are looming in many African countries. In Zambia teachers are increasingly dying of AIDS and for many teachers their teaching input is decreasing because they are sick. Swaziland estimates that it will have to train more than twice as many teachers as usual over the next 17 years just to keep the services at their 1997 levels. . . .

Economic Impact

There is growing evidence that as HIV prevalence rates rise, both total and growth in national income—gross domestic product, or GDP—

A teacher conducts a lesson in a Ugandan school. The prevalence of AIDS in Africa gravely threatens the quality of education in countries across the continent.

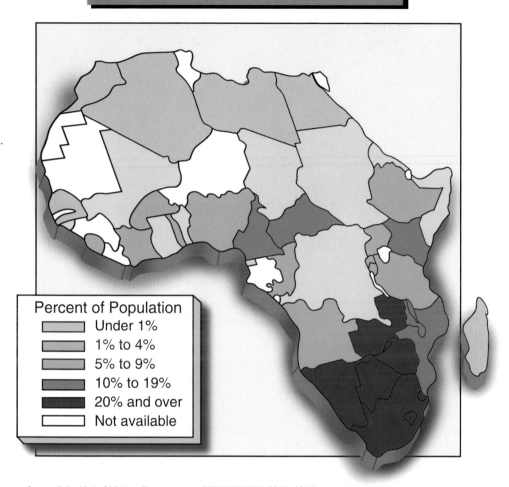

HIV in Africa: Percent of Population Aged 15–49 Infected with HIV

Percent of Population
- Under 1%
- 1% to 4%
- 5% to 9%
- 10% to 19%
- 20% and over
- Not available

Source: Joint United Nations Programme on HIV/AIDS/World Health Organization, 2002.

fall significantly. African countries where less than 5% of the adult population is infected will experience a modest impact on GDP growth rate. As the HIV prevalence rate rises to 20% or more, GDP growth may decline up to 2% a year.

In South Africa, the epidemic is projected to reduce the economic growth rate by 0.3–0.4% annually, resulting by the year 2010 in a GDP 17% lower than it would have been without AIDS and wiping US$22 billion off the country's economy. Even in diamond-rich Botswana, the country with the highest per capita GDP in Africa, in the next 10 years AIDS will slice 20% off the government budget,

Kenyan children infected with HIV eat a sugar compound as a dietary supplement. Many HIV-positive Africans suffer from severe malnutrition.

erode development gains, and bring about a 13% reduction in the income of the poorest households. . . .

Not Under Control

As the illness and death from AIDS rose in Africa, some two decades ago, one or two countries reacted quickly. Other countries waited rather longer before intensifying their efforts, but they too are being rewarded for their efforts. There have been a number of success stories which include Senegal, Uganda and Zambia. But most countries in Africa lost valuable time because AIDS was not fully understood and its significance as a new epidemic was not grasped. Some action was taken, but not on the scale that was required to stem the tide of the epidemic. . . .

Foreign Aid Is Imperative

Recently researchers have tried to determine how much money would be needed to make a real difference to the AIDS epidemic in Africa, and it is clear that scaling up the response to Africa's epidemic is not only imperative but it is affordable.

US$1.5 billion a year would make it possible to achieve massively higher levels of implementation of all the major components of successful prevention programmes for the whole of sub-Saharan Africa.

These would cover sexual, mother-to-child and transfusion-related HIV transmission, and would involve approaches ranging from awareness campaigns through the media to voluntary HIV counselling and testing, and the promotion and supply of condoms.

In the area of care for orphans and for people living with HIV or AIDS, costs depend very much on what kind of care is being provided. It is estimated that, with at least US$1.5 billion a year, countries in sub-Saharan Africa could buy symptom and pain relief (palliative care) for at least half of AIDS patients in need of it; treatment and prophylaxis for opportunistic infections for a somewhat smaller proportion; and care for AIDS orphans. At the moment, the coverage of care in many African countries is negligible, so reaching coverage at these levels would be an enormous step forward.

Making a start on coverage with combination anti-retroviral therapy would add several billion dollars annually to the bill.

Of course, providing AIDS prevention and care services involves more than just these funds. A country's health, education, communications and other infrastructures have to be well enough developed to be able to deliver these interventions. In some badly affected countries, these systems are already under strain, and they are likely to crumble further under the weight of AIDS. Then, too, money can only be used wisely if there are sufficient people available and the shortage of trained men, women and young is already acute.

These are some of the serious challenges that African countries and their partners in the global community will have to face if they are to make a real difference to the epidemic.

EVALUATING THE AUTHOR'S ARGUMENTS:

In this viewpoint AIDS Alert International describes the AIDS epidemic in Africa. What main points does the organization make about the disease in this continent? What evidence is offered to support each of these points? In your opinion, is this evidence convincing?

The African AIDS Epidemic Has Been Overstated

Rian Malan

"What if we wake up five years hence to discover that the [AIDS] problem has been blown up out of all proportion by unsound estimates?"

Estimates of AIDS cases in Africa are derived from flawed computer models, maintains Rian Malan in the following viewpoint, and are grossly inaccurate. He argues that while AIDS is a real problem in Africa, it is far less serious than researchers have stated. In fact, he reports, although researchers have predicted that huge numbers of Africans are infected and dying from AIDS, the population of Africa is actually increasing, not decreasing. According to Malan, much of the worldwide concern about AIDS is simply hysteria, based on unreliable estimates, and is causing Africa to receive millions of dollars in aid that could be better spent elsewhere. Malan is a journalist who has worked in both South Africa and the United States, and is author of *My Traitor's Heart.*

AS YOU READ, CONSIDER THE FOLLOWING QUESTIONS:
1. What does Botswana's census show about population growth there, according to Malan?
2. What population sample do computer models base their estimates on, as explained by the author?
3. According to Malan, why was Epimodel shelved in favor of ASSA 600?

I t was the eve of AIDS Day here [in Cape Town, South Africa]. Rock stars like Bono and Bob Geldof were jetting in for a fundraising concert with [former South African president] Nelson Mandela, and the airwaves were full of dark talk about megadeath and the armies of feral orphans who would surely ransack South Africa's cities in 2017 unless funds were made available to take care of them. My neighbour came up the garden path with a press cutting. 'Read this,' said Capt. David Price, ex–Royal Air Force flyboy. 'Bloody awful.'

It was an article from *The Spectator* describing the bizarre sex practices that contribute to HIV's rampage across the continent. 'One in five of us here in Zambia is HIV positive,' said the report. 'In 1993 our neighbour Botswana had an estimated population of 1.4 million. Today that figure is under a million and heading downwards. Doom merchants predict that Botswana may soon become the first nation in modern times literally to die out. This is AIDS in Africa.'

Population Actually Increasing

Really? Botswana has just concluded a census that shows population growing at about 2.7 per cent a year, in spite of what is usually described as the worst AIDS problem on the planet. Total population has risen to 1.7 million in just a decade. If anything, Botswana is experiencing a minor population explosion.

There is similar bad news for the doomsayers in Tanzania's new census, which shows population growing at 2.9 per cent a year. Professional pessimists will be particularly discomforted by developments in the swamplands west of Lake Victoria, where HIV first emerged, and where the depopulated villages of popular mythology are supposedly located. Here, in the district of Kagera, population grew at 2.7 per

Villagers cook fish over an open fire near Lake Victoria in Tanzania, the area where the first cases of HIV appeared.

cent a year before 1988, only to accelerate to 3.1 per cent even as the AIDS epidemic was supposedly peaking. Uganda's latest census tells a broadly similar story, as does South Africa's.

Some might think it good news that the impact of AIDS is less devastating than most laymen imagine, but they are wrong. In Africa, the only good news about AIDS is bad news, and anyone who tells you otherwise is branded a moral leper, bent on sowing confusion and derailing 100,000 worthy fundraising drives. I know this, because several years ago I acquired what was generally regarded as a leprous obsession with the dumbfounding AIDS numbers in my daily papers. They told me that AIDS had claimed 250,000 South African lives in 1999, and I kept saying, this can't possibly be true. . . .

Computer Projections

Who were they, these estimators? For the most part, they worked in Geneva for WHO [World Health Organization] or UNAIDS [Joint

United Nations Programme on HIV/AIDS] using a computer simulator called Epimodel. Every year, all over Africa, blood would be taken from a small sample of pregnant women and screened for signs of HIV infection. The results would be programmed into Epimodel, which transmuted them into estimates. If so many women were infected, it followed that a similar proportion of their husbands and lovers must be infected, too. These numbers would be extrapolated out into the general population, enabling the computer modellers to arrive at seemingly precise tallies of the doomed, the dying and the orphans left behind.

Because Africa is disorganised and, in some parts, unknowable, we had little choice other than to accept these projections. ('We' always expect the worst of Africa anyway.) Reporting on AIDS in Africa became a quest for anecdotes to support Geneva's estimates, and the estimates grew ever more terrible: 9.6 million cumulative AIDS deaths by 1997, rising to 17 million three years later.

These men operate a roadside coffin stand in Uganda. Despite the morbid implications of the photo, the populations of most African nations are actually increasing.

Or so we were told. When I visited the worst affected parts of Tanzania and Uganda in 2001, I was overwhelmed with stories about the horrors of what locals called 'Slims', but statistical corroboration was hard to come by. According to government census bureaux, death rates in these areas had been in decline since the second world war. AIDS-era mortality studies yielded some of the lowest overall death rates ever measured. Populations seemed to have exploded even as the epidemic was peaking.

Ask AIDS experts about this, and they say, this is Africa, chaos reigns, the historical data is too uncertain to make valid comparisons. But these same experts will tell you that South Africa is vastly different: 'The only country in sub-Saharan Africa where sufficient deaths are routinely registered to attempt to produce national estimates of mortality,' says Professor Ian Timaeus of the London School of Hygiene and Tropical Medicine. According to Timaeus, upwards of 80 per cent of deaths are registered here, which makes us unique: the only corner of Africa where it is possible to judge computer-generated AIDS estimates against objective reality.

Flawed Calculations

In the year 2000, Timaeus joined a team of South African researchers bent on eliminating all doubts about the magnitude of AIDS' impact on South African mortality. Sponsored by the Medical Research Council [MRC] the team's mission was to validate (for the first time ever) the output of AIDS computer models against actual death registration in an African setting. Towards this end, the MRC team was granted privileged access to death reports as they streamed into Pretoria. The first results became available in 2001, and they ran thus: 339,000 adult deaths in 1998, 375,000 in 1999 and 410,000 in 2000.

This was grimly consistent with predictions of rising mortality, but the scale was problematic. Epimodel estimated 250,000 AIDS deaths in 1999, but there were only 375,000 adult deaths in total that year—far too few to accommodate the UN's claims on behalf of the HIV virus. In short, Epimodel had failed its reality check. It was quietly shelved in favour of a more sophisticated local model, ASSA 600, which yielded a 'more realistic' death toll from AIDS of 143,000 for the calendar year 1999. . . .

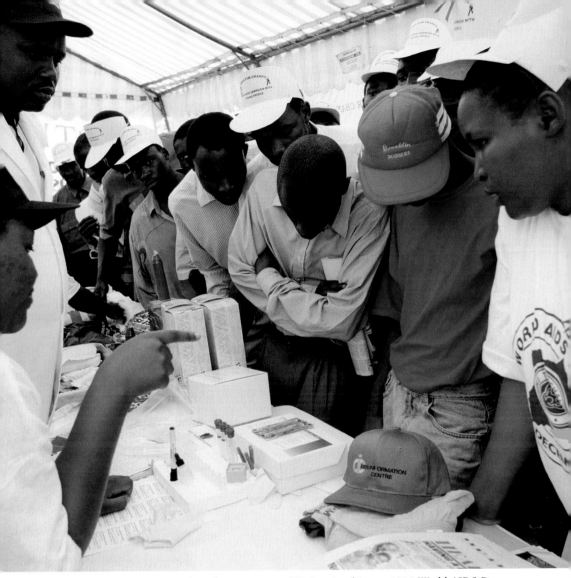

Ugandan health-care workers demonstrate an AIDS testing kit at a 1998 World AIDS Day event. Some people argue that such events only serve to fuel hysteria about the disease.

Towards the end of 2001, the vaunted ASSA 600 model was replaced by ASSA 2000, which produced estimates even lower than its predecessor: for the calendar year 1999, only 92,000 AIDS deaths in total. This was just more than a third of the original UN figure, but no matter; the boffins claimed ASSA 2000 was so accurate that further reference to actual death reports 'will be of limited usefulness'. A bit eerie, I thought, being told that virtual reality was about to render the real thing superfluous, but if these experts said the new model was infallible, it surely was infallible.

Only it wasn't. Last December [2002] ASSA 2000 was retired, too. A note on the MRC website explained that modelling was an inexact science, and that 'the number of people dying of AIDS has only now started to increase'. Furthermore, said the MRC, there was a new model in the works, one that would 'probably' produce estimates 'about 10 per cent lower' than those presently on the table. The exercise was not strictly valid, but I persuaded my scientist pal Rodney Richards to run the revised data on his own simulator and see what he came up with for 1999. The answer, very crudely, was an AIDS death toll somewhere around 65,000—a far cry indeed from the 250,000 initially put forth by UNAIDS.

FAST FACT

Since the early 1990s HIV infection rates in Uganda have steadily declined, from more than 30 percent to less than 6 percent in 2004.

A Computer Game

The wife has just read this, and she is not impressed. 'It's obscene,' she says. 'You're treating this as if it's just a computer game. People are dying out there.'

Well, yes, I concede that. People are dying, but this doesn't spare us from the fact that AIDS in Africa is indeed something of a computer game. When you read that 29.4 million Africans are 'living with HIV/AIDS', it doesn't mean that millions of living people have been tested. It means that modellers assume that 29.4 million Africans are linked via enormously complicated mathematical and sexual networks to one of those women who tested HIV positive in those annual pregnancy-clinic surveys. Modellers are the first to admit that this exercise is subject to uncertainties and large margins of error. Larger than expected, in some cases. . . .

The Need to Question AIDS Statistics

With such thoughts in the back of my mind, South Africa's AIDS Day 'celebrations' cast me into a deeply leprous mood. Please don't get me wrong here. I believe that AIDS is a real problem in Africa. Governments and sober medical professionals should be heeded when they express deep concerns about it. But there are breeds of AIDS activist and AIDS journalist who sound hysterical to me. On AIDS Day, they came forth like loonies drawn by a full moon, chanting that AIDS was getting worse and worse, 'spinning out of control', crippling economies, causing famines, killing millions, contributing to the oppression of women, and 'undermining democracy' by sapping the will of the poor to resist dictators. . . .

I think it is time to start questioning some of the claims made by the AIDS lobby. Their certainties are so fanatical, the powers they claim so far-reaching. Their authority is ultimately derived from computer-generated estimates, which they wield like weapons, overwhelming any resistance with dumbfounding atom bombs of hypothetical human misery. Give them their head, and they will commandeer all resources to fight just one disease. Who knows, they may defeat AIDS, but what if we wake up five years hence to discover that the problem has been blown up out of all proportion by unsound estimates, causing upwards of $20 billion to be wasted?

EVALUATING THE AUTHORS' ARGUMENTS:

Two of the authors in Chapter 1 claim that AIDS is a serious problem, while the other two contend that the seriousness of the AIDS epidemic has been greatly exaggerated. If you were to write an essay on the state of the global AIDS epidemic, what would be your opinion? What evidence would you use to support your case?

CHAPTER 2

How Can the Spread of AIDS Be Controlled?

Promoters of abstinence believe that it is the only way to stop sexually transmitted diseases.

VIEWPOINT

1

Abstinence-Only Education Is the Best Way to Prevent AIDS

Jerry Gramckow

"No one has ever caught AIDS . . . from being abstinent."

In the following viewpoint Jerry Gramckow argues that condoms do not provide youths with sufficient protection from AIDS because young people are often spontaneous and forgetful and are likely to use them incorrectly. In his opinion, a more successful strategy against AIDS is abstinence education. He believes that youths have proven to be capable of abstinence if they receive sufficient motivation and support. Gramckow is a contributing writer for Focus on the Family, an organization that works to preserve traditional values and the institution of the family.

AS YOU READ, CONSIDER THE FOLLOWING QUESTIONS:
1. According to Gramckow, what does the Youth Risks Behavior Survey show about youth abstinence?
2. What did a 2001 government report show about the effectiveness of condoms against HIV/AIDS, as cited by Gramckow?
3. According to one study, as cited by the author, what percentage of sexually active people always use a condom?

Q. *Since most teens are sexually active, shouldn't schools teach the majority how to protect themselves with condoms, rather than catering to the minority who abstain?*

Capable of Abstaining

A. No. The truth is, most teens are not sexually active. The latest survey from the Centers for Disease Control and Prevention (CDC) shows that teen sexual activity has been declining steadily over the last seven years (since about the time abstinence programs really took hold [approximately 1996]). The CDC's 2001 Youth Risks Behavior Survey found that fewer than 43 percent of our nation's teens had ever engaged in sexual intercourse, and just one-third said they are "currently sexually active." Clearly, teens are capable of abstaining from sex; they just need the right motivation and support.

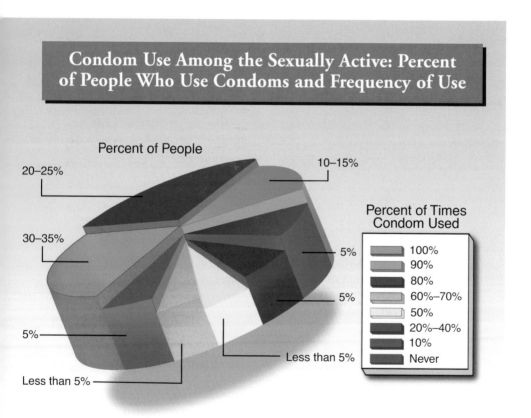

Condom Use Among the Sexually Active: Percent of People Who Use Condoms and Frequency of Use

Percent of People

20–25%

10–15%

30–35%

Percent of Times Condom Used

5%

	100%
	90%
	80%
	60%–70%
	50%
	20%–40%
	10%
	Never

5%

5%

Less than 5%

Less than 5%

Source: International AIDS Foundation, 2003.

Insufficient Protection

Q. But doesn't abstinence-only education leave that one-third who are sexually active—which is still a sizeable minority—unprotected and vulnerable?

A. Granted, kids who engage in "unprotected" sex are vulnerable to sexually transmitted diseases (STDs) and unwanted pregnancies. But this raises another crucial question: How much protection do condoms provide? Studies have found condom failure rates in protecting against pregnancies for teens to be as high as 22.5 percent. As for protecting against STDs, in 2001 several government health agencies together released a report on condom effectiveness. The report found evidence that condoms are about 85 percent effective in preventing the spread of HIV/AIDS. (Is 85 percent good enough in protecting your child against a deadly and incurable virus?) The report also found condoms to be somewhat effective in protecting men (but not women) from gonorrhea. But the prominent scientists who prepared the report found no conclusive evidence that condoms protect against any other STD, including HPV [human papillomavirus], the primary cause of cervical cancer, which kills more women than AIDS does. Sixty-eight million Americans now have an incurable STD. Many caught those incurable STDs while using condoms. No one has ever caught AIDS or any other STD from being abstinent. Who's really more vulnerable, the teen taught to use condoms or the one who's motivated to save sex for marriage?

> **FAST FACT**
>
> The U.S. Centers for Disease Control and Prevention issued a national health objective for 2010: to increase the proportion of adolescents in grades nine through twelve who have never had sexual intercourse.

Kids Are Forgetful

Another crucial point to remember is that kids are notoriously spontaneous and forgetful. (How many times have you reminded your teen to take his jacket to the football game as he rushed from the

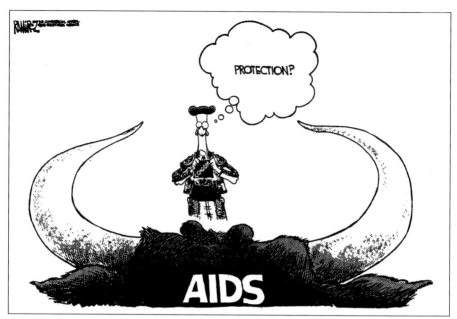

Source: Ramirez. © 1993 by Copley News Service. Reproduced by permission.

house?) The CDC has stated that for condoms to be effective they must be used "every time you have sex—100 percent of the time—no exceptions." One study found that only about 13 percent of sexually active people always use a condom. That figure may be even worse for teens. In the heat of passion kids are likely to forget the eight-step process for proper condom use.

EVALUATING THE AUTHORS' ARGUMENTS:

List three main points that Jerry Gramckow makes to prove his case that abstinence is the only way to prevent AIDS. How do you think AIDS Action, the author of the next viewpoint, would reply to these arguments?

Abstinence-Only Education Will Not Prevent AIDS

AIDS Action

"Abstinence-only programs do not provide young people with the information . . . they may need to protect themselves from HIV infection."

Youths need comprehensive sexual education that includes both abstinence and safe sex practices, maintains the advocacy group AIDS Action in the following viewpoint. The organization insists that it is not realistic to promote abstinence only because some youths will engage in sexual activity. It argues that these youths must be educated about how to prevent HIV infection. In addition, the organization points out, no evidence supports fears that educating youths about sex will increase sexual activity. The evidence actually shows that sexual activity may decrease with education. AIDS Action is a national organization dedicated to the analysis and development of sound policies and programs in response to the AIDS epidemic.

AS YOU READ, CONSIDER THE FOLLOWING QUESTIONS:

1. What percentage of high school seniors report having had sex by graduation, according to AIDS Action?

Each year, half of all new HIV infections in the United States are among individuals under age 25. Two young Americans under the age of 25 are infected with HIV every hour, resulting in 20,000 new infections per year among young people. Yet federal funding trends support abstinence-only education rather than comprehensive abstinence and sexual health education programs that prepare teenagers for the world outside their classrooms. By graduation, 65 percent of all high school seniors report having had sex. Full knowledge of the options available to adolescents, from abstinence to safer sex, is important in empowering young people, influencing the choices they make about sex, and preventing new HIV infections. Abstinence-only programs do not meet the needs of America's youth in their quest for the information and skills necessary to make good decisions and stay healthy.

FAST FACT

A 2002 study conducted by a researcher at Columbia University found that students who made virginity pledges were one-third less likely than others to use protection when they did have sex for the first time.

While abstinence-only programs focus exclusively on abstaining from sexual activity until marriage, abstinence-plus programs seek to educate individuals about all facets of sexual health with a focus on abstinence. Information regarding the prevention of sexually transmitted diseases (STDs), including HIV, is discussed in addition to highlighting the option of abstaining from sexual activity until marriage. Research has shown that comprehensive sex education programs that discuss both abstinence and protection from sexually transmitted diseases actually delay the onset of sexual intercourse, reduce the frequency of intercourse, and reduce the number of sexual partners.

Abstinence-Plus Education Works

Comprehensive sexuality education that advocates abstinence yet provides education for those teens that choose to become sexually active has proven practical and effective. Abstinence-plus education, which provides a range of information and options for young people from abstinence to safer sexual behavior, does not increase sexual activity or lower the age of a young person's first sexual encounter. There is no evidence that abstinence-only education is effective in preventing or delaying sexual activity. In fact, a recent abstinence-only initiative in California actually resulted in more students reporting sexual activity after participating in the program.

Concerns that discussing explicit sexual information with youth would result in an increase in sexual activity or early initiation of sex among youth have proven unfounded. A recent Institute of Medicine (IOM) report supported abstinence-plus programs, citing studies that found that teens with comprehensive sexuality education were less likely to engage in sexual intercourse, and those who had sex did so less often and were more apt to use protection.

A group of teenagers promotes abstinence at a rally in New York.

Surveys have shown that an overwhelming majority of parents want their children to receive information about sex, including both abstinence and contraception, from trained professionals at schools. Parents who engage their children in frank discussions of STD and HIV risk are quite effective: A study of mother-adolescent communication regarding HIV demonstrated an increase in condom use only for teens whose mothers had talked to them about condoms before they became sexually active. Similarly, a survey of 522 African-American adolescent girls found that those girls who regularly discussed sex with their parents were significantly less likely to engage in behavior that placed them at risk for HIV and much more likely to bring up STD/HIV prevention with sexual partners than girls whose parents did not discuss sex, STDs, and HIV.

Current Trends and Programs

Comprehensive sexuality education helps to minimize behavior that places adolescents at risk for HIV, and it is in demand among American

A Connecticut high school student speaks to younger students about the importance of abstinence. The number of schools implementing abstinence-only education programs is increasing.

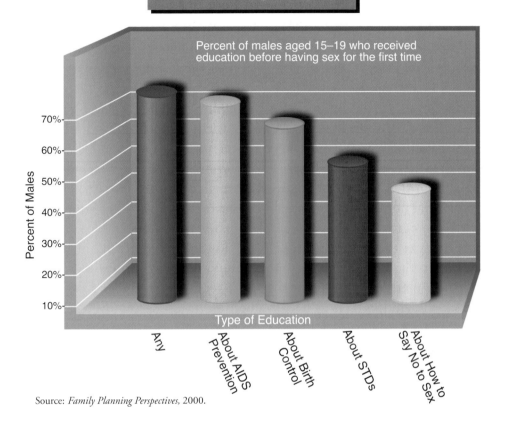

Knowledge Gap

Percent of males aged 15–19 who received education before having sex for the first time

Percent of Males

70%
60%
50%
40%
30%
20%
10%

Type of Education

Any / About AIDS Prevention / About Birth Control / About STDs / About How to Say No to Sex

Source: *Family Planning Perspectives,* 2000.

youth. Most teens know about HIV transmission, but they want to know more about protecting themselves against HIV. Today's teens need information about sexual behavior and HIV/AIDS. The Kaiser Family Foundation has found that 68 percent of all sexually active teens did not think they were personally at risk of contracting HIV. However, 65 percent of sexually active teens are personally concerned about HIV/AIDS.

According to the IOM and the Presidential Advisory Council on HIV/AIDS, a significant challenge in preventing HIV transmission among teens is the increasing number of abstinence-only sex education programs in schools. These programs are offered in place of comprehensive or abstinence-plus sex education programs. Additionally, in his recent [2001] *Call to Action,* [former] Surgeon General David Satcher asserted, "given that one-half of adolescents in the United States are already sexually active—and at risk of unintended pregnancy and

STD/HIV infection—it also seems clear that adolescents need accurate information about contraceptive methods so that they can reduce those risks." There is no evidence to support the widespread adoption of abstinence-only programs, whereas providing teens with more information has been found to delay the initiation of sexual activity and promote better overall health.

Currently [2001] most (35) states require sexuality education to be taught in school. In 11 of those states, the curriculum must focus on abstinence until marriage, with brief mention of STD and HIV prevention. In two of those states, HIV prevention education is only discussed in the context of abstinence until marriage. In three of the states that do not require sexuality education, if it is taught voluntarily, the program can only discuss abstinence until marriage. The number of states requiring abstinence-only education is growing. In 1988, two percent of public school teachers reported teaching abstinence as the sole method of protection against sexually transmitted diseases (STDs) including HIV. That number rose to 23 percent by 1999.

Comprehensive Sexual Education Is Needed

There is a growing trend of providing abstinence-only education at the expense of comprehensive sexual education that includes abstinence as well as pregnancy, STD, and HIV prevention. Abstinence-plus programs provide teenagers with a range of options and information. With half of all new HIV infections in the U.S. each year occurring among teens and young adults, more information about HIV prevention could prevent additional infections. Abstinence-only programs do not provide young people with the information or negotiation skills that they may need to protect themselves from HIV infection.

EVALUATING THE AUTHOR'S ARGUMENTS:

Compare the different examples and statistics that AIDS Action uses to support its contention that abstinence-only education will not prevent AIDS. Rank them in order of most convincing to least convincing.

The U.S. Emergency Plan for AIDS Relief Can Fight AIDS

"Under the Emergency Plan . . . money is being used well, to extend lives and reduce the suffering caused by HIV/AIDS worldwide."

Randall L. Tobias

The following viewpoint is excerpted from "Ask the White House," an online interactive forum where questions from members of the public are presented, and answered by government officials. Randall L. Tobias, coordinator of United States Government Activities to Combat HIV/AIDS Globally, discusses the U.S. Emergency Plan for AIDS Relief, a five-year plan in which the United States has pledged $15 billion over five years—beginning in 2004—to fight AIDS worldwide. Tobias maintains that under this plan, the United States is investing extensive resources for research and prevention around the world. He asserts that the U.S. plan is balanced and effective, and is helping countries such as those in Africa make progress in the fight against AIDS.

Randall L. Tobias, "Ask the White House," www.whitehouse.gov, December 1, 2004.

AS YOU READ, CONSIDER THE FOLLOWING QUESTIONS:
1. According to Tobias, under its five-year plan, how much money will the United States contribute toward combating AIDS?
2. What does the author mean when he says, "We must provide both fish and fishing poles"?
3. What is "the whole premise" of the Emergency Plan, according to Tobias?

*P*erry, *from Santa Rosa writes:* What kind of positive things has the President done for AIDS? I hear he is criticized for not giving enough money, but I remember a few years back in his State of the Union that he pledged lots of money to Africa and AIDS funding. Is this still true? Is it going on?

Ambassador Randall L. Tobias:

Perry, thanks for your interest. Yes, the President did pledge lots of money to fight global AIDS . . . and he's following through on that pledge. His Emergency Plan for AIDS Relief is the largest commitment ever by a nation toward an international health initiative for a single disease—a five-year, $15 billion, multifaceted approach to combating the disease in more than 100 countries around the world.

Under the Emergency Plan, America is working with our partners in-country and supporting national strategies, by providing $2.4 billion this past year [2004]

> **FAST FACT**
>
> According to the AIDS Advocacy Coalition, between 1998 and 2004, the AIDS vaccine budget of the U.S. National Institutes of Health increased from $148 million to $463 million.

(the first year of the plan), and even more this coming year. That money is being used well, to extend lives and reduce the suffering caused by HIV/AIDS worldwide.

Under President [George W.] Bush, the focus is no longer on the hurdles we face in fighting this disease. We are now urgently employing the best practices available to fight this disease and bring hope. We're laying the groundwork for a sustained, successful effort.

ABC Policy

Beth, from Alameda, CA writes:

How is promoting only abstinence going to stop the spread of AIDS, especially when much of it is spread through trafficking and prostitution?

Ambassador Randall L. Tobias:

Beth, I'm so glad you asked this question, because it gives me a chance to clear up a lingering misconception about President Bush's Emergency Plan. A key element of our strategy is the balanced ABC policy, pioneered with tremendous success in Uganda. It does include an emphasis on 'Abstinence' especially for youth, but also on 'Being faithful,' especially for those in committed relationships, and for those who engage in risky behavior, it includes correct and consistent use of 'Condoms.' Those are the A, B and C of ABC.

And our prevention work doesn't start and end with ABC. As I mentioned earlier, we are also providing drug therapy and intensive counseling to prevent mother-to-child transmission of HIV. We also support locally designed behavior change strategies that direct tailored messages to appropriate groups, support the roles of parents and others who can help protect girls, and strengthen families' and communities' ability to care for orphans and vulnerable children.

The U.S. is also partnering with communities to find solutions to such issues as sexual coercion and exploitation of women and girls, as well as fighting sex trafficking and prostitution, while still serving victims of these activities.

To ensure that the problems women face are addressed from every angle, the President's Emergency

Randall L. Tobias, a government health official, argues that the United States has dedicated significant resources to the battle against the AIDS epidemic.

Plan also includes highly successful relationship and anti-violence programs aimed at men and boys to help them develop healthy relationships with women.

So the U.S. policy is not a limited, one-size-fits-all policy. It is a balanced, science-based one that focuses on what works.

Striking a Balance

Joel, from Salem, Oregon writes:

Amb. Tobias—Can the US simply continue giving these countries that are struggling with AIDS more and more help? It seems that at some point we need to begin teaching them how to deal with AIDS, so that eventually they will be able to better fight AIDS themselves, with minimal US or international help. Thank-you.

Ambassador Randall L. Tobias:

Joel, thanks, I'm glad for the insightful question! We simply must help the nations that have taken the heaviest blow from HIV/AIDS

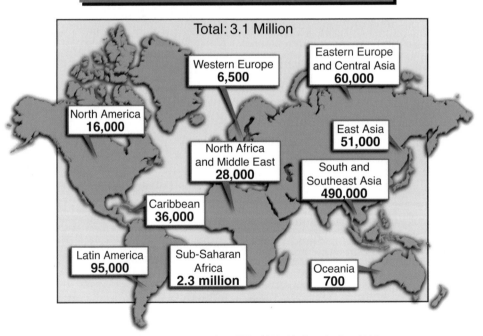

Estimated Adult and Child Deaths from AIDS in 2004

Total: 3.1 Million

Western Europe
6,500

Eastern Europe and Central Asia
60,000

North America
16,000

East Asia
51,000

North Africa and Middle East
28,000

South and Southeast Asia
490,000

Caribbean
36,000

Latin America
95,000

Sub-Saharan Africa
2.3 million

Oceania
700

Source: Joint United Nations Programme on HIV/AIDS/World Health Organization, 2004.

During pregnancy, this South African mother unwittingly infected her daughter with HIV. Part of President Bush's AIDS plan seeks to reduce the number of mother-to-child infections.

develop their own capabilities to address the crisis. In places like Africa, the Caribbean, and Southeast Asia, there is a desperate lack of health care workers and infrastructure. For example, Mozambique has only 500 doctors to serve a population of 18 million people! The reality is that all the AIDS drugs in the world won't do any good if they're stuck in warehouses, unable to be delivered to those in need. The way I sometimes put it is that we must provide both fish and fishing poles.

So President Bush's Emergency Plan is working closely with our partners in the hardest-hit nations in support of the national strategies. For example, we're helping provide health care infrastructure and supporting training programs. This year, the Emergency Plan is supporting 145 antiretroviral therapy-focused training programs, and an additional 140 programs focusing on palliative care, in the 15 countries where we are placing a special focus. It's not easy, but we are striving to strike the right balance between meeting the immediate needs of today and helping nations develop the capability to handle the needs of the future. . . .

Striving for a Cure
Chris, from Rancho Palos Verdes, CA writes:
    Do you think we will see a cure for AIDS in our lifetime?

While touring Haiti as part of a mission to raise global awareness about AIDS, Randall L. Tobias presents an AIDS patient with his first dosage of antiretroviral drugs.

Ambassador Randall L. Tobias:

Chris, I wish I could give you an answer—and even more, that the answer would be "very soon." But I simply do not know. What I do know is that America is making a tremendous investment in doing the scientific research that might lead to both a vaccine and a cure. The other thing I know is that while we wait for a vaccine and a cure, we must use all the tools currently available to us to defeat HIV/AIDS. That means using effective prevention programs to keep people safe in the first place. It means making lifesaving antiretroviral drugs available to people in the developing world. It means caring for the orphans and the others affected by HIV/AIDS. These activities are the focus of President Bush's Emergency Plan, even as our nation's vaccine and cure research activities continue.

No Time for Complacency
Cliff, from Brimfield, Ohio writes:

Ambassador Tobias: Not long ago you could not pick up a newspaper or watch the news without hearing something about HIV/AIDS.

Has this issue been placed on the back burner with the war [against terrorism] and all going on? You don't even hear of it anymore; it's as if a cure all has been found. I know of course that's not so. So just where are we in fighting HIV/AIDS? Are we gaining ground or like the drug war, losing ground? With the issue out of sight it kind of gets out of mind also. So just what are the most recent facts and figures? Thank You.

Ambassador Randall L. Tobias:

Cliff, complacency is a deadly enemy in this fight, and I share your concern. The facts are these: no cure for HIV/AIDS has yet been found. In the world last year, 3 million people died of AIDS— that's 8000 people a day. And in that same year, 5 million people became newly infected. So if you do the math, it is apparent that it would be madness to put the fight against HIV/AIDS on the "back burner."

At the level of the U.S. government, I'm pleased to report that there is absolutely no complacency in responding to this killer. President Bush sees HIV/AIDS as the global menace it is, and the whole premise of his Emergency Plan for AIDS Relief is that this is an unprecedented emergency requiring an unprecedented response. But it is crucial that all of us as individual citizens continue to take HIV/AIDS seriously. With 8000 people dying each day, time is not on our side.

EVALUATING THE AUTHORS' ARGUMENTS:

In the viewpoint you just read, the author believes the U.S. Emergency Plan for AIDS Relief is a good way to fight AIDS. The author of the next viewpoint disagrees. After reading both viewpoints, what is your opinion about the plan? Cite from the text to support your argument.

The U.S. Emergency Plan for AIDS Relief Is Ineffective

Stephen Gloyd

"Most of the PEPFAR [President's Emergency Plan for AIDS Relief] money actually ends up in U.S. hands rather than going to Africans."

Under the U.S. Emergency Plan for AIDS Relief, the United States has pledged to spend $15 billion over five years—beginning in 2004—to fight AIDS worldwide. This plan is not an effective way to fight AIDS, argues Stephen Gloyd in the following viewpoint, because very little of the money provided by the United States will actually end up going to Africans or their institutions—the major recipients of the plan. Instead, says Gloyd, the poor African countries receiving the money will pay a large portion of it back to rich countries in debt repayments. Another large portion of the money will go back to the United States to purchase AIDS drugs, he maintains, leaving Africa with little money with which to fight AIDS. Gloyd is director of the International Health Program at the School of Public Health and Community Medicine at the University of Washington.

AS YOU READ, CONSIDER THE FOLLOWING QUESTIONS:
  1. According to the author, why does the U.S. government not like to give money directly to African governments?
  2. How much of the PEPFAR aid value actually goes to the recipient country, in Gloyd's opinion?
  3. As stated by the author, what is the first alternative to PEPFAR?

By all appearances, the Bush administration is finally providing real money to fight AIDS in Africa. Sure, the $15 billion "PEPFAR" program (President's Emergency [Plan] For AIDS Relief) is under attack for buying expensive brand name drugs rather than cheap and equivalent generic drugs.

A South African woman holds a sign at a rally in Johannesburg to protest the amount of money the U.S. government has pledged to combat the AIDS epidemic.

Moreover, President [George W.] Bush is criticized for demanding that PEPFAR AIDS programs focus on abstinence and faithfulness in a context where such a focus might be ineffective. Nevertheless, the administration is credited by most critics as having provided an enormous amount of resources to fight AIDS, said to be more than double the sum of all other donor support worldwide in 2004.

How It Really Works

The untold part of this story is where the money flows are going. Most of the PEPFAR money actually ends up in U.S. hands rather than going to Africans or their institutions. Worse still, over the past two decades, African governments have been paying $15 billion per year in debt installments to donors and banks in the rich countries of the north. The sum effect is that poor countries of Africa are subsidizing the rich countries while the rich country governments are putting aid money into their home-country organizations in the name of poor Africans.

Here's how it works. The U.S. government doesn't like to give money directly to African governments. Why? Part of it is political and philosophical. Ever since the [former U.S. president Ronald] Reagan era, the government officially has preferred supporting the private sector rather than governments. Another reason is that these governments are said to have inadequate "absorptive capacity," that is, the health ministries don't have adequate management and financial systems to account for the money; the health clinics don't have enough trained health care providers to provide the services; and their health clinics are lacking equipment and are poorly maintained. The public sector in Africa literally has been crumbling away for the past two decades.

Ironically enough, a big reason for the crumbling governments comes from U.S. policies—debt repayment schemes called Structural Adjustment Programs. These programs are austerity measures imposed

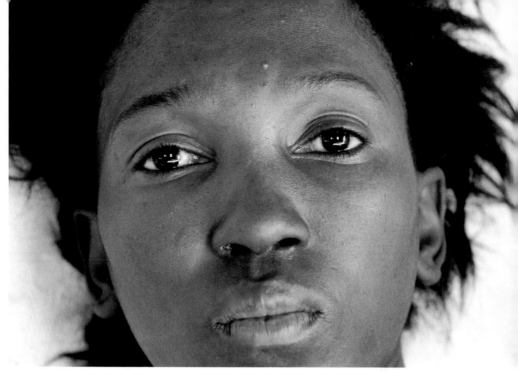

Unable to afford AIDS treatment, this severely weakened South African woman is confined to her bed. Most of the PEPFAR money fails to reach the Africans who need it.

on nearly every African government to squeeze public money to pay their debts to foreign banks. Most people don't know that the debts came about mostly because of factors external to African governments. The big factors are enormously high interest rates (up to 22 percent)—caused by U.S. financial policies—that increased payments; and U.S. and European subsidies that decreased prices of African exports.

Even with debt reduction schemes, debt repayments continue largely unabated. Poor-country money is sent away—money that could cover all AIDS treatment costs, improve crumbling health services and provide much-needed funds for other basic services in countries whose populations live under $1 per person per day.

Where the Money Goes

So who gets the PEPFAR money? Most of the money goes to U.S.-based non-governmental organizations. We now know that a big chunk of the money lets them buy AIDS drugs from U.S. drug companies, who make a significant profit on PEPFAR by charging four to five times what it would cost to buy equivalent generic drugs. Most of the remaining money goes for expensive salaries and benefits to foreign

During a 2004 demonstration, AIDS activists, including U2 front man Bono (foreground), call on President Bush and Randall Tobias to make generic AIDS drugs available.

(usually U.S.) staff, their very nice cars and offices, their operating expenses and overhead costs to support their home offices in the United States. Though the accounting is difficult, it is likely that less than 25 percent of PEPFAR aid value actually goes to recipient-country people or institutions. The money actually making it to an African country might be even less if profits to drug companies are counted as going back to the United States.

The result: Of the $15 billion of PEPFAR funds, African governments will be lucky to see $3 billion to $4 billion over five years [2004–2009]. At the same time they will be paying $75 billion back to rich countries in debt repayments. The money that is being paid back is "real" money—money that can be spent on local people and institutions.

Debt Forgiveness and External Support

Is there an alternative? Absolutely. The first thing to do is to forgive the debt, using the same arguments the administration is using to justify forgiving the debt in Iraq.

Debt forgiveness will liberate a huge sum of money that can go to training and hiring more Africans for public jobs; to pay living-wage salaries; to buy medicines and to improve conditions at hospitals, clinics and schools. In 2001, when Mozambique's debt was cut in half, the health budget doubled and health-worker salaries moved up to livable range. The second alternative is to provide external support through institutions that can provide money to local agencies in Africa, both government and civil society. Institutions already exist that can channel such money much more efficiently than PEPFAR. The Global Fund to Fight AIDS, Tuberculosis and Malaria is one such example that is creating a new paradigm for international assistance. Sad to say, the administration is proposing cutting its contribution by 60 percent this year.

The time to act is now. [Musician] Bob Dylan asked "How many deaths will it take till we know that too many people have died?" Enough have died already.

> **EVALUATING THE AUTHOR'S ARGUMENTS:**
>
> What pieces of evidence does the author of this viewpoint use to back up his argument that Africa is unlikely to benefit from PEPFAR? Do you find this evidence convincing? Explain.

VIEWPOINT 5

Efforts to Control AIDS Should Focus on Poverty

Peter Mann

"AIDS is being spread by impoverishment, by deadly patterns of development that make people poor."

Peter Mann is the coordinator of World Hunger Year, an organization dedicated to fighting hunger and poverty through community-based solutions. In the following viewpoint he argues that AIDS is spread by poverty. This is evident, says Mann, in groups such as women and African Americans, where the rates of both AIDS and poverty are highest. He believes that the patterns of development in poor communities cause the spread of AIDS, and that this increase in AIDS leads to a further increase in poverty. In Mann's opinion, to be effective, any response to AIDS must work to rebuild communities and reduce impoverishment.

AS YOU READ, CONSIDER THE FOLLOWING QUESTIONS:

1. As explained by the author, what happens as AIDS moves through poor African American communities?
2. What percentage of women in sub-Saharan Africa are infected with HIV/AIDS, according to Mann?
3. In the author's opinion, how does labor migration contribute to AIDS in West Africa?

The latest AIDS news [in 2001] is terrifying. One in every 50 Black American men may be infected with HIV, according to the Centers for Disease Control.

Globally, more than 50 million people have been infected, and more than 20 million have already died.

Dr. Peter Piot, executive director of UNAIDS [Joint United Nations Programme on HIV/AIDS] a consortium of U.N. agencies fighting the pandemic, says 36 million are currently infected.

Africa, home to only nine percent of the world's population, has two-thirds of current AIDS infections, and AIDS will claim the lives of around one-third of today's 15-year-olds in Africa. Yet the greatest risk of a new AIDS explosion lies in Asia, home to 60 percent of the world's population.

Until now, almost all public responses have been to treat AIDS as a medical problem, and an issue of high-risk behavior—the sharing of infected needles by drug users, and unprotected sex within at-risk communities.

A Poverty Issue

What is coming more clearly into view, as the pandemic reaches into every region of the globe, is that AIDS is more than a health crisis or

Two homeless women in Washington, D.C., sleep on a park bench. Among the nation's poor, there is an extremely high incidence of AIDS.

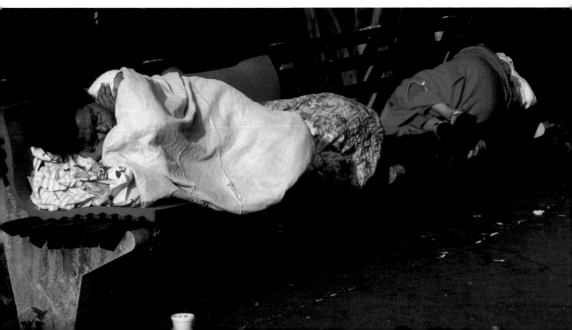

a lifestyle issue. AIDS is also a crisis of poverty. Poverty spreads AIDS. And, in turn, the widening AIDS crisis increases poverty. In fact, it would be even more accurate to say that AIDS is being spread by impoverishment, by deadly patterns of development that make people poor and place at risk whole sectors of populations.

AIDS Among African Americans and Women

In the United States, the alarming spread of AIDS within the African-American community has been concentrated within the inner cities, targeting the poor and the addicted. People in these inner-city poor neighborhoods are marginalized, often malnourished, in poor health, and without adequate health care for prevention or treatment.

A nurse in a New York hospital cares for an HIV-positive African American baby. Inner-city African Americans find themselves at an inordinately high risk for HIV infection.

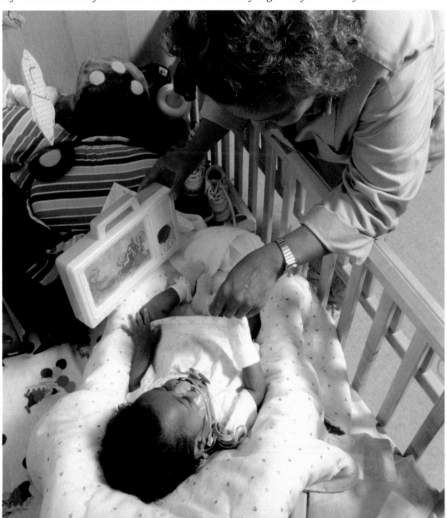

A poor South African woman prepares a meal over an open fire. Women and girls represent an increasing proportion of those infected with HIV in Africa.

While high-risk behavior in these communities directly spreads HIV/AIDS, urban poverty is clearly a contributing cause. And as AIDS moves through these communities, they become still poorer and more marginalized.

The figures are startling. In 1999, African Americans were less than 13 percent of the U.S. population, more than 26 percent of the poor, and 37 percent of all reported cases of HIV/AIDS.

By 2000, AIDS had become in the U.S. the leading cause of death for Blacks between the ages of 25 and 44. Yet these communities reflect the realities of global poverty, where 1.2 billion people live on less than one dollar a day, lack basic health care, education, adequate food and clean water, and are increasingly marginalized—impoverished—within the global economy.

The status of women is a key indicator of vulnerability to AIDS.

Women and girls are a majority of the world's poor, and they represent an increasing proportion of those infected by HIV/AIDS—55 percent in sub-Saharan Africa.

Women in the developing world are often malnourished, vulnerable to infections and sexually transmitted diseases, without health care, and lacking power inside the family. Thus they are placed in a high-risk environment for AIDS.

Responses to Poverty

Rural impoverishment is a root cause of labor migration in West Africa, which brings AIDS back into home communities; of commercial sex work in the cities of Thailand by which women support rural households; of professional donors in China who make a little extra money by selling their blood into an unsafe blood system.

All of these are high-risk behaviors that spread AIDS; but they are also responses to a social and economic system of development that deprives the poor of choices. Public policy decisions also deprive the poor of treatment.

India spends only about one percent of its GDP [gross domestic product] on health care, and China less than 1 percent. Zambia, where one out of nine citizens are HIV-infected, spends more on debt servicing than on health care.

The Need to Address Poverty

The AIDS news is frightening. Social collapse is an evident danger in countries whose doctors, teachers, farmers—and parents—are dying. It is, therefore, a sign of hope that U.N. agencies, as well as some governments, are beginning to respond to AIDS as a crisis that intensifies poverty. But governments are not yet responding to new research showing that poverty and inequality themselves are root causes of the AIDS crisis. Still less are they willing to change this development pattern. Yet AIDS is a poverty issue in every sense. If this crisis is to be solved, national policies are needed to rebuild communities and reform public health.

EVALUATING THE AUTHOR'S ARGUMENTS:

What main ideas does Peter Mann use to support his theory that AIDS is caused by poverty? In your opinion, is reducing poverty an effective way to reduce AIDS? Why or why not?

Efforts to Control AIDS Should Target the Promiscuous

Albert-Laszlo Barabasi

"The best hope lies in helping the promiscuous few, not the heart-rending many."

In the following viewpoint Albert-Laszlo Barabasi points out that because money to fight AIDS is limited, decisions must be made about where to spend it most effectively. He makes a case for giving AIDS drugs and other aid to the most sexually promiscuous members of society rather than children and others who arouse public sympathy. While this may seem cruel, says Barabasi, it is the only effective way to eradicate the disease, because these promiscuous people are the ones spreading it through their webs of sexual contacts. Barabasi is a physics professor at the University of Notre Dame in Indiana and author of *Linked: The New Science of Networks*.

AS YOU READ, CONSIDER THE FOLLOWING QUESTIONS:

1. What did the author's study of the World Wide Web reveal about hubs?
2. According to Barabasi, how do hubs play a key role in spreading a virus?
3. What important ethical question does the author admit that his policy raises?

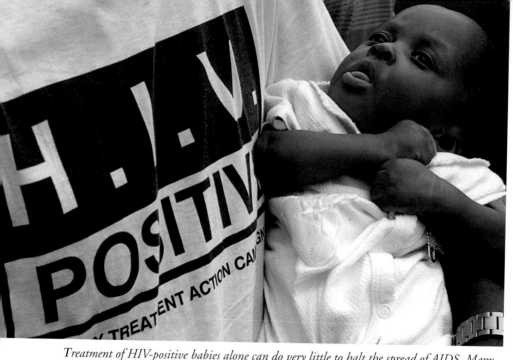

Treatment of HIV-positive babies alone can do very little to halt the spread of AIDS. Many argue that efforts to combat AIDS must target those who have promiscuous sex.

With Congress seriously considering a historic escalation in the global battle against AIDS,[1] nobody seems to want to talk about a profound ethical dilemma: How should the money be spent?

Help the Few to Save Many

With a stunning 8,000 new HIV infections a day, doing something is clearly a moral imperative. AIDS activists and public-health workers advocate increasing the distribution of condoms to stop the disease's spread and making drugs widely available to help the victims. And on Capitol Hill, a coalition is forming around AIDS as a children's issue, with politicians across the ideological spectrum supporting the distribution of drugs that prevent mothers from passing AIDS to their unborn children.

Yet, in the campaign to eradicate the worst plague of the modern era, all these approaches are common-sensical, compassionate—and doomed. The insights of a burgeoning field of science—the theory of networks—combined with hard lessons from the front lines suggest

1. This refers to the U.S. Emergency Plan for AIDS Relief, a five-year, $15 billion U.S. initiative to fight AIDS, which began in 2004.

that the best hope lies in helping the promiscuous few, not the heart-rending many.

Decades of epidemiological studies have assumed that viruses spread on a social network in which individuals randomly interact with each other. In the past few years, though, we have learned that networks are far from random.

Hubs and AIDS

My research group, studying the World Wide Web, discovered that it has a peculiar, nonrandom structure: A few popular hubs, such as Yahoo or Google, link many small Web pages together. In the broader world, the same pattern repeats itself. A few key molecules in our cell's complex

Pakistani prostitutes demand that their government implement free AIDS testing.

chemical web interact with a staggering number of other molecules to keep us alive.

A handful of large corporations—the economic hubs that have financial ties to thousands of other companies—dominate our economy.

Hubs, it turns out, are what make networks so resilient.

These discoveries have profound implications for understanding how AIDS spreads and how to stop it.

Recently, a team of Swedish and American scientists mapped a network of sexual contacts, a kind of "sex web." They found the same kind of hub structure seen in other networks; although most people have one to 10 sexual partners during their lifetime, a few individuals, such as Wilt Chamberlain,[2] collect thousands.

At the same time, Italian theorists have offered a shocking prediction: In networks dominated by hubs, even a disease like AIDS—which is not highly infectious—will persist and spread.

Hubs play a key role in spreading a virus: They are likely to become infected because of their many sexual contacts and, once infected, are likely to spread it to many people.

> **FAST FACT**
>
> Between 1991 and 2003 Thailand reduced its annual cases of HIV infection from 140,000 to 21,000, by routinely testing sex workers for the disease, and by vigorously promoting condom use to these workers and their customers.

While the use of condoms may save the individual, they will never eradicate the epidemic. Nor will drugs, if not given to all.

A Difficult Solution

Given limited resources, the unique role of the hubs suggests a bold but cruel solution: When there is not enough money to help everybody who needs it, we should primarily give it to the hubs. Indeed, if we identify and help all the individuals who have many potential sexual partners, the number of newly infected cases will drastically decrease. The more hubs we target, the higher the chance that the epidemic will die out.

---

2. American basketball player who claimed to have had sex with more than twenty thousand women

The sexual behavior of prostitutes like these Indian women helps to spread AIDS and other sexually transmitted diseases to the larger population.

An effective AIDS policy requires more than money for drugs. We need the resources to quickly identify the hubs, and then we must have the mandate to single them out. Epidemiologists have long known the important role that prostitutes play in spreading sexually transmitted diseases. What the new science of networks is telling us is that any AIDS policy that ignores them is destined to fail.

Such a policy that targets individuals, of course, raises important ethical questions. Should society "reward" promiscuity? But with so many people dying every day, the real question is this: What is the best way to save the most people?

EVALUATING THE AUTHOR'S ARGUMENTS:

In the viewpoint you just read, Albert-Laszlo Barabasi uses the theory of hubs to explain his contention that AIDS prevention efforts should target the promiscuous. What evidence does he offer to prove that the theory is applicable to the AIDS epidemic? Do you think this evidence is sufficient? Why or why not?

Efforts to Control AIDS Should Focus on Developing a Vaccine

"The best long-term hope for controlling the AIDS epidemic . . . is the development of . . . HIV vaccines."

U.S. Department of Health and Human Services

The following viewpoint is excerpted from a publication by the U.S. Department of Health and Human Services, the federal agency responsible for protecting the health of all Americans and providing essential human services. The agency maintains that HIV and AIDS are serious worldwide problems and that despite the availability of treatment drugs, the development of a vaccine is the best long-term hope for controlling the AIDS epidemic. According to the agency, in order to develop such a vaccine, there must be increased research and community participation in vaccine drug trials.

AS YOU READ, CONSIDER THE FOLLOWING QUESTIONS:
1. When was the value of vaccines first recognized, according to the author?

U.S. Department of Health and Human Services, "HIV Vaccines Explained: Making HIV Vaccines a Reality," www.aidsinfo.nih.gov, February 2004.

2. What type of participants are needed in HIV vaccine trials, as argued by the U.S. Department of Health and Human Services?
3. As cited by the author, how many new HIV infections occur each day?

A preventive HIV vaccine is a substance that teaches the body's immune system to recognize and protect itself against HIV, the virus that causes AIDS. HIV vaccines currently being tested in humans are made from man-made materials that **CANNOT** cause HIV infection.

Scientists believe that an effective HIV vaccine, given before exposure to HIV, could have a number of possible outcomes. These include:

- Preventing infection in most people
- Preventing infection in some people

A research scientist works in the lab to develop an AIDS vaccine. Many people are confident a vaccine will be developed in the very near future.

- Preparing a person's immune system to block continued infection and eliminate the virus (vaccines against measles, mumps and polio work this way)
- Delaying or preventing the onset of illness or AIDS

The long-term goal is to develop a vaccine that is 100 percent effective and protects everyone from infection. However, even if a vaccine only protects some people, it could still have a major impact on controlling the epidemic. A partially effective vaccine could decrease the number of people who get infected with HIV; those people, in turn, would not pass the virus on to others. Even when an HIV vaccine is developed, education and other prevention efforts will be needed so that people continue to practice safe behaviors.

History of Vaccines

The value of vaccines was recognized approximately 200 years ago, beginning with a vaccine against smallpox. The smallpox vaccine saved millions of lives, and its success helped people understand that introducing a vaccine into the body can actually trigger a protective immune response, and prevent disease.

Today, there are numerous safe and effective vaccines. Vaccines have been used successfully against many life threatening diseases, including measles and polio in most of the world.

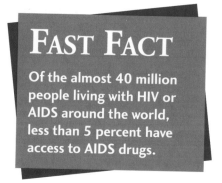

FAST FACT

Of the almost 40 million people living with HIV or AIDS around the world, less than 5 percent have access to AIDS drugs.

Community Participation in Vaccine Research

By raising awareness and encouraging study participation, individuals and communities can contribute to the successful development of HIV vaccines. Although tens of thousands of people have already volunteered to take part in HIV vaccine studies, many more will be needed. A large HIV vaccine trial will require thousands more participants of all races/ethnicities, genders and socioeconomic backgrounds to ensure that the vaccine works in all populations.

Therefore, community support is essential in efforts to break down stigma and myths about HIV vaccine research. Developing an effective HIV vaccine depends upon individuals and communities informing, educating and supporting others. . . .

The Need for an HIV Vaccine

Despite the availability and success of HIV treatment drugs in the United States, the best long-term hope for controlling the AIDS epidemic worldwide is the development of safe, effective and affordable preventive HIV vaccines. Consider these facts:

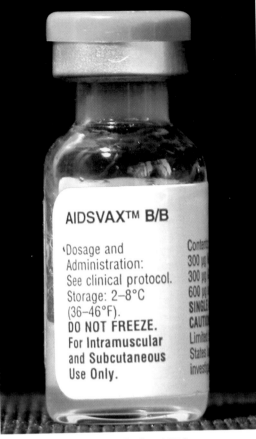

Although AIDSVAX and other AIDS vaccines have proven ineffective, the prospects for an effective vaccine are improving.

HIV/AIDS in the United States

- Nearly half a million Americans have died of AIDS since the epidemic began.
- The Centers for Disease Control and Prevention (CDC) estimate that as many as 950,000 Americans are living with HIV, and more than one-third of them do not know it.
- Each year, over 40,000 people become infected with HIV, a rate that has remained virtually unchanged in recent years. Seventy percent are men and 30 percent are women. Of these, half are younger than 25 years of age.
- Minority communities are disproportionately affected by the epidemic. More than half of all new HIV infections occur in African Americans, who make up 12 percent of the U.S. population. AIDS is the fifth leading cause of death of Americans aged 25–44, and is the number one cause of death in African American men of all ages. Nineteen percent of new HIV infections occur in Latinos, who make up 13 percent of the population.

AIDS vaccine researchers examine a plate used to measure immune cells. An HIV vaccine will allow a person's immune system to recognize and protect itself against HIV.

HIV/AIDS around the world

- To date [2004], nearly 25 million men, women and children have died from AIDS worldwide.
- Currently, 40 million people are estimated to be living with HIV/AIDS and 14,000 new infections occur each day.
- Today, more than 13 million children under the age of 15 have lost one or both of their parents to AIDS, most in sub-Saharan Africa.

Preventive Versus Therapeutic HIV Vaccines

Preventive HIV vaccines currently under development are given to HIV negative people and are designed to prevent infection and control the spread of HIV, not to cure AIDS.

Multiple HIV vaccines may be necessary to prevent infection or disease in the same way multiple drugs are needed to treat people already infected with HIV.

Researchers are also evaluating therapeutic vaccines to treat people with HIV infection or AIDS. While the same vaccine may be tested for both preventive and therapeutic effects, what works to prevent HIV infection may not necessarily work to treat people who are already infected with HIV.

Is an HIV Vaccine Available Now?
No! Scientists have been studying HIV for over two decades—and continue to make progress. Even when a promising vaccine is discovered, it will take time to test and evaluate its safety and effectiveness.

Testing HIV Vaccines
Vaccine development requires several years of research in laboratories and animals before testing in humans can begin. A potential vaccine goes through three phases of testing in humans before the Food and

A man participates in an AIDS vaccine trial in Philadelphia. To be effective, clinical trials of AIDS vaccines must be conducted in different populations and regions.

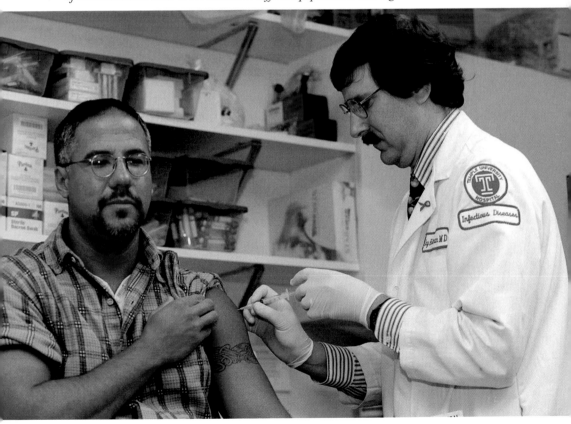

Drug Administration (FDA) can consider licensing it for public use. The three phases of preventive HIV vaccine clinical trials are:

- *Phase I*—involves a small number of healthy volunteers (HIV-negative) to test the safety and various doses of the vaccine; usually lasts 12 to 18 months
- *Phase II*—involves hundreds of volunteers (HIV-negative) to test the safety and immune responses of the vaccine; can last up to 2 years
- *Phase III*—involves thousands of volunteers (HIV-negative) to test the safety and effectiveness of the vaccine; can last 3 to 4 years

Throughout all phases of human testing, independent reviewers regularly monitor the study to ensure the safety of the volunteers. . . .

So far, few side effects have been associated with experimental HIV vaccines. Those that have occurred generally have been mild to moderate and similar to those of approved vaccines.

EVALUATING THE AUTHORS' ARGUMENTS:

Because there are limited resources with which to combat AIDS, decisions must be made about where to use them. Peter Mann, Albert-Laszlo Barabasi, and the U.S. Department of Health and Human Services all have different opinions about how these resources could be most successfully used to fight AIDS. How do you think the money would best be used? Cite from the viewpoints to back up your answer.

CHAPTER 3

How Should AIDS in Africa Be Addressed?

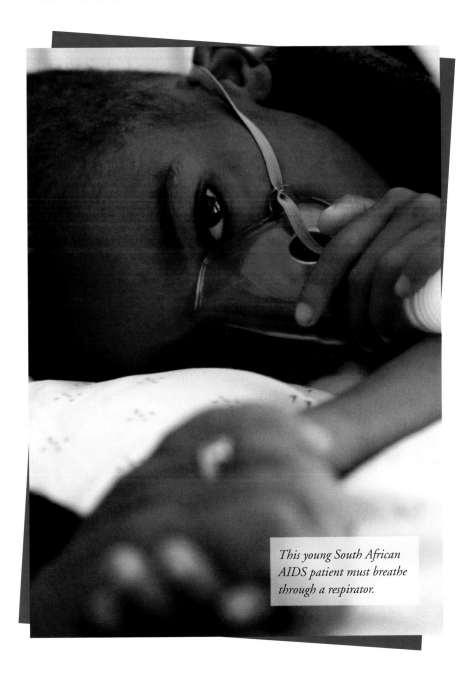

This young South African AIDS patient must breathe through a respirator.

Condoms Will Help Prevent AIDS in Africa

Human Rights Watch

"Condoms are not a complete solution to the spread of HIV, but they are a necessary tool to combat that spread."

Human Rights Watch is a U.S.-based human rights organization that conducts investigations into human rights abuses in all regions of the world. In the following viewpoint the organization argues that condoms are scientifically proven to help reduce the spread of AIDS and that condom use should be encouraged in countries around the world, including Africa. Unfortunately, alleges Human Rights Watch, rather than helping to promote condoms, the United States—a leading donor of AIDS funds—and many influential political and religious leaders have encouraged abstinence instead. As a result of this pressure to teach abstinence, many African countries are reducing their promotion of condoms and putting their populations at risk for AIDS. In order to reduce the rate of AIDS, condoms must be used, states the organization.

AS YOU READ, CONSIDER THE FOLLOWING QUESTIONS:

1. In addition to interfering with public health, how do restrictions on condoms impact human rights, according to Human Rights Watch?

2. Under the Emergency Plan for AIDS Relief, what percentage of AIDS prevention spending is devoted to abstinence programs, as cited by the author?
3. According to Human Rights Watch, in 2003, what percentage of people at risk for HIV had access to condoms?

HIV/AIDS is a preventable disease, yet approximately 5 million people were newly infected with HIV in 2003, the majority of them through sex. Many of these cases could have been avoided, but for state-imposed restrictions on proven and effective HIV prevention strategies, such as latex condoms. Condoms provide an essentially impermeable barrier to HIV pathogens. According to the Joint United Nations Programme on HIV/AIDS (UNAIDS), scientific data "overwhelmingly confirm that male latex condoms are highly effective in preventing sexual HIV transmission." However, many governments around the world either fail to guarantee access to condoms or impose needless restrictions on access to condoms and related HIV/AIDS information. Such restrictions interfere with public health as well as set back internationally recognized human rights—the right to the highest attainable standard of health, the right to information, and the right to life.

Restrictions on Lifesaving Information

In the midst of this crisis, the world's leading donor to HIV/AIDS programs, the United States, has ramped up its support for HIV prevention programs that promote sexual abstinence and marital fidelity. The United States Leadership against AIDS, Tuberculosis and Malaria Act of 2003 (commonly known as the President's Emergency Plan for AIDS Relief or PEPFAR) devotes 33 percent of prevention spending to "abstinence until marriage" programs, concentrating these programs on fifteen heavily AIDS-affected countries in sub-Saharan Africa, the Caribbean and Asia. As implemented domestically in the United States, government-funded "abstinence only" programs censor science-based information about condoms and suggest that heterosexual marriage is the only reliable strategy for prevention of sexually transmitted HIV. Abstinence-only programs do not provide a proven effective alternative to programs that include accurate information about condom use, and may cause harm. . . .

It is not only the United States that restricts access to condoms and lifesaving information about HIV/AIDS. In many countries, political and/or religious leaders have made public statements associating condoms with sin or sexual promiscuity, implying that people who use condoms lack the moral fortitude to abstain from sex until marriage. . . .

A Necessary Tool to Combat AIDS
Given these restrictions, it should come as no surprise that the vast majority of people at risk of HIV lack the basic tools to protect themselves from this fatal disease. In 2003, fewer than half of all people at risk of sexual transmission of HIV had access to condoms. Less than one quarter had access to basic HIV/AIDS education. The United Nations Population Fund (UNFPA) estimated in 2000 that over 7 billion additional condoms were needed in developing countries to achieve a significant reduction in HIV infection. International funding for procuring condoms declined throughout the 1990s, and U.S.

A billboard on a Zambian street promotes AIDS awareness. Educating people about AIDS and condom use is a powerful tool in the fight against the disease.

condom donations remain well below levels seen in the early 1990s despite recent reported increases. At the same time, U.S. funding for international "abstinence until marriage" programs increased exponentially in 2003 with the enactment of PEPFAR.

Condoms are not a complete solution to the spread of HIV, but they are a necessary tool to combat that spread. . . . While abstinence and fidelity may work for some people in some cases, promoting these behaviors at the expense of condoms deprives people of complete information and services for HIV prevention. To avert this health and human rights crisis, governments and international donors should immediately lift any restrictions on access to condoms and take concrete steps to guarantee comprehensive and science-based HIV-prevention services to all those who need them. . . .

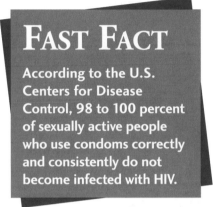

FAST FACT

According to the U.S. Centers for Disease Control, 98 to 100 percent of sexually active people who use condoms correctly and consistently do not become infected with HIV.

A Harmful Trend in Africa

Following the ramping up of U.S.-funded "abstinence until marriage" programs, leaders of African countries standing to receive PEPFAR funding made numerous public statements in favor of sexual abstinence as a primary HIV prevention strategy. In May 2004, for instance, Ugandan president Yoweri Museveni deviated from his historical support of condoms by stating that condoms should be provided only for sex workers. This change in position occurred at approximately the same time that the U.S. announced that Uganda would receive $90 million of PEPFAR funds. President Museveni continued to make similar statements in his public speeches, including at the International AIDS Conference in July 2004.

There are signs of attitudes towards condoms changing elsewhere as well. In Zambia, President Mwanawasa gave a speech in 2004 suggesting that traditional methods to fight HIV/AIDS, including promoting condoms and public awareness campaigns, were not working

Orphans of the AIDS virus, a fifteen-year-old Zambian girl takes care of her younger sister. An estimated 12 million children in sub-Saharan Africa have been orphaned due to AIDS.

and that the country needed instead to promote sexual abstinence. In March 2004, the Zambian government reportedly banned the distribution of condoms in schools on the grounds that condoms promoted promiscuity among youth.

In Swaziland, which has one of the highest HIV prevalence rates in the world (between 37 and 40 percent of adults as of 2004), leading government officials and important public figures, including the founder of Swaziland's AIDS Support Organization, took public anti-condom stands in 2003. A top traditional leader reportedly ridiculed condoms as ineffective and inconsistent with "Swazi manhood." In 2001, the Kenyan government discontinued the supply of free condoms to the general population, although it continued to supply highly subsidized condoms. When asked about this change, a health ministry official stated that if the poor cannot afford condoms, they should be faithful. . . .

Access to Condoms Is Vital
Human Rights Watch calls on all governments, donors to HIV/AIDS programs, and relevant United Nations bodies to take the following broad steps to guarantee access to condoms and HIV/AIDS information. . . .

Publicly counter misinformation about condom safety and efficacy. Issue clear statements setting out the effectiveness of condoms against

U.S. government health official Randall Tobias meets with Ugandan children to discuss AIDS prevention. Sadly, few African children are properly educated about the transmission of AIDS.

HIV/AIDS and clear instructions for their correct and consistent use. Publicly counter false or misleading statements about the effectiveness of condoms against HIV. Withhold public funds from organizations that make false or misleading statements about condoms. Support programs that guarantee comprehensive information about HIV prevention, including information about the effectiveness of condoms.

Take steps to expand HIV prevention services that include condoms. Work with relevant government agencies, nongovernmental organizations, the private sector, and social marketing groups to ensure adequate supply of condoms in health facilities and in commercial outlets. Develop and implement comprehensive HIV/AIDS education programs that explicitly recognize the effectiveness of condoms against HIV. Withhold public funds from programs that give emphasis to abstinence and fidelity at the expense of condom information and services.

EVALUATING THE AUTHORS' ARGUMENTS:

In the viewpoint you just read, Human Rights Watch argues that condoms are an important part of AIDS prevention in Africa. In the next viewpoint, Pete Winn contends that abstinence and faithfulness, not condoms, should be promoted in Africa. After reading both viewpoints, what is your opinion? Use evidence from the text to support your position.

Condoms Will Not Prevent AIDS in Africa

Pete Winn

"There is little evidence that condoms are having an effect [against AIDS in Africa]."

In the following viewpoint Pete Winn asserts that while AIDS is a serious problem in Africa, condoms are not the way to combat it. According to Winn, there is no evidence that condom use is reducing the spread of AIDS in Africa, while there is increasing evidence that abstinence and monogamy are. He cites Uganda as an example, where he believes AIDS rates have decreased due to an emphasis on marital fidelity and abstinence. Condoms, he maintains, are not the answer to Africa's AIDS problem. Winn is an associate editor for Focus on the Family, an organization that seeks to preserve traditional values and the institution of the family.

AS YOU READ, CONSIDER THE FOLLOWING QUESTIONS:

1. In the author's opinion, how were traditional morality and abstinence viewed at the 2002 International AIDS Conference in Spain?
2. In a 1991 speech, what did Ugandan president Yoweri Kaguta Museveni call for, as cited by Winn?
3. According to the author, what happened to HIV prevalence rates in Uganda between 1991 and 2001?

Every year, "The Hunger" arrives in Southern Africa—it usually begins at the end of January and lasts a couple of months. Always relief workers find malnourished, emaciated children with distended stomachs, discolored hair and skin dropping off their bones—the heart-breaking and horrifying pictures of major famine we have all seen. . . .

Why are an estimated 12.8 million people at risk of dying—more than ever before? Several reasons: environment, bad crops, government corruption. But arguably the worst reason is also a relative newcomer: AIDS.

"In Malawi, one in every five members of the population are HIV-positive," [Clive] Calver [head of World Relief, the relief arm of the National Association of Evangelicals] said. "That means that often the parents are dead, and the children are now facing death because of the famine. There was a bad harvest this year, and a bad harvest last year, and children are eating the crops green and they're eating the seed."

AIDS has become an enormous problem in Africa. And it affects far more than just famine. According to UNAIDS [Joint United Nations Programme on HIV/AIDS], a United Nations umbrella group which includes five U.N. agencies, the World Bank and the World Health Organization, 34.3 million people in the world have AIDS—24.5 million of them in sub-Saharan Africa. In addition, nearly 19 million have died from AIDS—3.8 million of them children under the age of 15—and 13.2 million children have been orphaned by AIDS, 12.1 million of them in Africa.

The Wrong Answer

At the recent [2002] International AIDS Conference in Barcelona, Spain, condoms and "safe-sex" practices were promoted as the answer to the pandemic, especially in Africa. Traditional morality, abstinence and other faith-based efforts to combat AIDS took a beating.

For instance, as University of Zimbabwe Professor Paul Gundani recited a list of the people in his family recently struck down by AIDS, he did so in front of a poster which said, "Because the bishops ban condoms, innocent people die."

"My sister (died) last week, and my brother last year," the 42-year-old Roman Catholic theologian recounted. "By now, my nephew may be dead, too."

Former South African President Nelson Mandela also told the conference that "enlightened" AIDS practices were needed in Africa.

An executive with the producers of "Sesame Street"—the children's television series that is popular around the world—even announced at the AIDS conference plans to introduce an HIV-positive Muppet on the South African version of the show, in order to help address the problem.

Ugandan women hold hands at an AIDS counseling center. Nearly 25 million people in Uganda and other sub-Saharan nations are afflicted with AIDS.

What was not mentioned in Barcelona, however, was the fact that there is little evidence that condoms are having an effect, while the evidence is mounting that abstinence and traditional morality do have an impact.

"Unfortunately, some nations in Southern Africa—especially South Africa—are still promoting the safe-sex myth that condoms can stop the pandemic," said Jerry Gramckow, an abstinence expert at Focus on the Family. "They can't."

Uganda: AIDS Success Story

What does work? Indeed, while HIV/AIDS infection rates in many African countries are increasing, Gramckow pointed out that the rates in some African nations—notably Uganda—actually have been decreasing dramatically. Why? Abstinence.

At the 2002 International AIDS Conference in Barcelona, Spain, Bill Clinton applauds the efforts of Nelson Mandela to halt the spread of AIDS in South Africa.

A billboard in Malawi promotes abstinence as a way to prevent the spread of AIDS. In recent years, abstinence programs in some African countries have been successful.

While some try to credit condoms for the improvement, Dr. Edward C. Green, of the Harvard School of Public Health, does not.

Green, who examined the Ugandan experience scientifically, wrote in a recent report: "Few in public health circles really believed—or even believe nowadays—that programs promoting abstinence, fidelity or monogamy, or even reduction in number of sexual partners, pay off in significant behavioral change. My own view of this changed when I evaluated HIV prevention programs in Uganda and Jamaica."

Green said that when Ugandan President Yoweri Kaguta Museveni began to enlist help from religious organizations in 1992, many secular AIDS workers thought abstinence education programs would have few, if any, measurable results.

Indeed, in a November 1991 speech, Museveni called for a return to "old-fashioned" morals.

"I have been emphasizing a return to our time-tested cultural practices that emphasized fidelity and condemned premarital and extramarital sex," he said.

Could a return to "old-fashioned" morals significantly reduce the HIV/AIDS epidemic in Uganda? According to Green, HIV prevalence rates dropped 70 percent between 1991 and 2001.

He added in his study: "Some reports continue to claim that the world's great success story in AIDS prevention, Uganda, owes its achievement to condoms, but this is not true."

In fact, the Uganda AIDS Commission policy specifically recommended the following steps:

- Seek prompt treatment for any STD (sexually transmitted disease) infection and have regular check-ups.
- Have self-confidence and esteem skills as a method of preventing AIDS.
- Practice safe behavior, which involves:
  - Abstaining from sex before and outside of marriage.
  - Avoiding drugs and alcohol.
  - Avoiding people who are bad influences.

Condom use was not listed among the commission's recommendations. Indeed, as Dr. Vinand Nantulya, an infectious-disease specialist, pointed out in his analysis of the Uganda plan: "Ugandans never took to condoms."

Nantulya credits Uganda's "zero-grazing"—or marital fidelity—campaign as the major reason for Uganda's success in fighting HIV/AIDS. Green added that according to the Demographic and Health Survey, 95 percent of all Ugandans age 15 to 49 now report practicing monogamy or abstinence.

EVALUATING THE AUTHORS' ARGUMENTS:

The author of this viewpoint does not believe that condom use should be encouraged as a way to fight AIDS in Africa. How do you think Human Rights Watch, the author of the previous viewpoint, might respond to this argument?

Africa Needs AIDS Drugs

Edward Susman

Millions of Africans are dying unnecessarily, argues Edward Susman in the following viewpoint, because they are being denied access to the AIDS drugs that could save their lives. According to Susman, world leaders have failed to help provide these drugs because of beliefs that Africans will not use them properly and that they will become less diligent in trying to prevent the disease. These beliefs are myths, he maintains; AIDS drugs can, and should, be immediately provided to Africans. Susman is a medical journalist.

"Few people in [the] underdeveloped world have obtained access to the drugs that can save their lives"

AS YOU READ, CONSIDER THE FOLLOWING QUESTIONS:

1. In Susman's opinion, what has been the result of funding promises by wealthy nations?
2. What have studies in Senegal and Uganda proven about AIDS drugs, according to the author?
3. According to Jean-Paul Moatti, as quoted by Susman, why do AIDS drugs make good economic sense?

While world leaders spent this past week [July 2003] in Paris talking about creating a "war chest" to fight AIDS, in Soweto and Durban and Nairobi people just died, suffering and waiting in silence for the drugs that could have saved them.

The Global Fund to Fight AIDS, Tuberculosis and Malaria is crying for donations. Greece, a country of 10.6 million, has agreed to pledge only $250,000 for the campaign that is trying to save 7 million people from dying this year from the three epidemics.

Waiting for Drugs

As another 15,000 people—mostly in Africa—took their final, tortured breaths today, leaders of the global fund, meeting in conjunction with the 2nd International AIDS Society Conference, tried to round up capital to pay for projects in more than 90 countries.

Among the dead were people like Rwassa, a young African woman infected with HIV—the AIDS virus. Her health began to deteriorate in 2001, but because she worked with an AIDS organization in Burundi, she knew of international promises by the wealthiest nations to fund treatments in the poorest nations. So she assumed their promises would be fulfilled.

FAST FACT

According to the World Health Organization, only 1 percent of the millions of Africans who need AIDS drugs receive them.

She had hoped therapy would become available for her, said Dr. Marie-Josee Mbuzenakamwe of Bujumbura, Burundi, the young woman's colleague. She hoped the AIDS war chest would be funded to provide the antiretroviral medication she needed.

"The G8 countries have had no trouble making speeches that do justice to the seriousness of the epidemic," Mbuzenakamwe said in her keynote speech to the AIDS conference, and referring to the group composed of some of the world's economic powers—the United States, Canada, Germany, Italy, Japan, the United Kingdom, France and Russia. "Not one of those countries has respected its commitments," she charged.

An HIV-positive South African woman campaigns in her community on behalf of the efficacy of antiretroviral drug therapy.

Rwassa held on until March 2002. "When she died she was still talking about the drugs that would come to save her life," Mbuzenakamwe said.

Those drugs did not arrive and the war chest remains unfilled. . . .

Myths About Treatment

Few people in [the] underdeveloped world have obtained access to the drugs that can save their lives, even though 90 percent of the disease occurs in those nations. AIDS persists not only because of lack of funds but because of barriers in the minds of bureaucrats and doctors who have allowed myths about treatment to prevail.

Jean-Paul Moatti, professor of economics at the University of the Mediterranean in Marseilles, France, said many of the difficulties of not getting drugs to underdeveloped countries involve these myths.

For example, he said, scientists have raised concerns that if patients do not adhere to their antiretroviral treatment regimens, it could create worldwide resistant strains of HIV that could make fighting the disease worse.

Such worries ignore the evidence, Moatti said, "that demonstrate viral resistance and non-adherence to treatment are no greater problems in . . . patients in Africa than in developed countries." He said the argument employs a double standard: The prospect of antiretroviral resistance and non-compliance by patients are no barriers for treating rich Americans and Europeans, but somehow they are barriers to treating poor Africans and Asians.

The myth quoters, Moatti said, ignore studies in African countries such as Senegal and Uganda that have proven patients in poorer settings take their medication, just as they do in resource-rich countries.

For example, a new study examining resistance patterns in Europe concluded as many as 10 percent of new AIDS infections among Europeans are caused by viral resistance—compared to only about 3 percent among African patients.

Moatti said because generic copies of antiretroviral cocktails[1] can lower the cost of drug treatments dramatically, which makes it cost-effective, even in the poorest of countries, to give the drugs to AIDS patients.

"Access to anti-retroviral therapy is not just a moral imperative," Moatti said. "It is good economic sense." He said treatment with the drugs will result in cost savings by keeping people out of hospitals. It also will prevent opportunistic infections[2] from developing, thereby requiring more drugs as well as hospitalization.

Endless Debate and Insufficient Coordination

He said one myth haunting delivery of drugs in Africa has been the debate over whether prevention and therapy can be delivered simultaneously. The fear is if people knew they could obtain treatment, they would not be diligent in trying to avoid the disease. In fact, Moatti said his research shows treatment availability actually enhances testing, condom use and prevention measures.

"We have an economic rationale now," said Dr. Michel Kazatchkine, director of the Agence nationale de recherches sur le sida, the French national AIDS research organization.

---

1. An antiretroviral cocktail is a combination of drugs that prolong and improve the quality of life for people with HIV or AIDS. 2. Because a person with HIV has a weak immune system, they are prone to a wide range of infections that a healthy person's body could normally fight off.

Source: Mill. © by Mill Newsart Syndicate. Reproduced by permission.

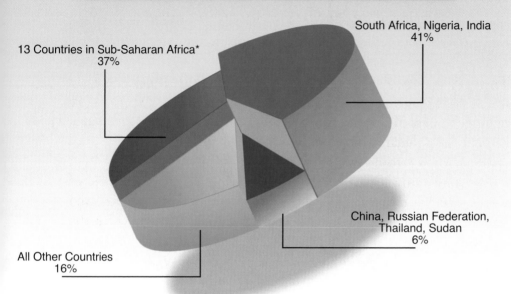

AIDS Drugs Needed: 5.1 Million People Worldwide Need AIDS Treatment

South Africa, Nigeria, India
41%

13 Countries in Sub-Saharan Africa*
37%

China, Russian Federation, Thailand, Sudan
6%

All Other Countries
16%

Percent of 5.1 million, by region

Source: World Health Organization, 2004.   * Other than South Africa and Nigeria

"Three years ago people were still thinking we should go to prevention rather than treatment," he said. "Then people were saying the drugs were too expensive. Then people were saying the drugs were not cost-effective. Then people were saying we don't know if the drugs will be effective in the context of the developing world."

At this week's AIDS conference, Kazatchkine told UPI [United Press International], "we believe we are bringing evidence to fight against all of these arguments."

Not that the fault lies entirely with the nations with money, Kazatchkine continued. "There are obstacles. There is insufficient commitment among those in the developed world and in the governments of underdeveloped nations."

For example, in South Africa, despite offers to provide drugs to prevent the transmission of the disease from pregnant mothers to their babies, treatment programs still are difficult if not impossible to find in Durban and the eastern part of the country, where the epidemic is greatest.

"There is insufficient coordination within the countries between the civil societies and the governments and the health sectors and financial sectors," Kazatchkine said at a news briefing. "There is insufficient manpower. But even with the available manpower we should be able to scale up treatment programs much better than we currently do."

Dying from a Treatable Disease

The debate goes on, about the myths and about the money—how much should be given to the global fund and when to give it. As the talk continues, so do the deaths: 3 million from AIDS each year, 2 million from malaria and 2 million from tuberculosis.

All are dying from diseases for which there are treatments.

Mbuzenakamwe said she lives with two realities: "One made of words, which is ultimately meaningless, for the words are not followed by results; and the other—the one in which we live—in which the numbers of deaths and infected people grow every day."

She predicted the global fund meeting would fail to provide meaningful additions to the global fund coffers. True to her prediction, the meeting failed to provide anything meaningful.

Millions of people in Africa and the rest of the underdeveloped world need action now. In the time it took to read this article, about 10 people in sub-Saharan Africa died from AIDS.

The speeches go on in Paris, in Washington and elsewhere. In Africa, the speeches are at the funerals of those who are dying while the rest of the world turns away.

EVALUATING THE AUTHORS' ARGUMENTS:

Edward Susman, the author of this viewpoint, and Pete Winn, the author of the previous viewpoint, offer different arguments on how AIDS can best be reduced in Africa. After reading these viewpoints, can you think of any points these authors might agree on regarding AIDS in Africa? Explain.

VIEWPOINT
4

AIDS Drugs Will Not Solve Africa's AIDS Problem

Robert Baker

"If they were to give away the drugs to combat HIV, AIDS would continue to kill millions in Africa."

Robert Baker is a specialist registrar in infectious diseases and HIV medicine in a London teaching hospital. In the following viewpoint he argues that even if AIDS drugs were provided free to Africans, the AIDS problem there would not be solved. In order to be successful, these drugs must be taken according to a strict regimen, and patients need expensive support facilities to monitor their treatment. While this is possible in many Western nations, such as Britain, says Baker, Africa lacks the resources to do this. As a result, he maintains, not only would the drugs be incorrectly and ineffectively used, but drug-resistant strains of HIV might develop. Baker advocates the development of an AIDS vaccine as the best solution for Africa.

AS YOU READ, CONSIDER THE FOLLOWING QUESTIONS:

1. What happens if you do not take AIDS drugs properly, as explained by the author?

2. According to Baker, what is now a major cause of HIV morbidity and mortality?
3. In the author's opinion, why do almost none of the HIV vaccine researchers work for drug companies?

The South African President, Thabo Mbeki, is right to say that
HIV is not responsible for the spread of AIDS in Africa.
Poverty is. The pharmaceutical companies are regularly condemned for being unscrupulous and money-grubbing, but the fact is
that if they were to give away the drugs to combat HIV, AIDS would
continue to kill millions in Africa. Indeed, if the drugs were free, the
death toll might rise.

This is not to suggest that Mr Mbeki has got his science right. You
cannot contract AIDS without infection from HIV. There is really no
doubt at all that it is the agent which so catastrophically destroys the

*South African president Thabo Mbeki maintains that poverty is the dominant factor
responsible for the spread of AIDS throughout Africa.*

immune systems of infected individuals. There are a few scientists, chief among them the American Alan Duesberg, who say that it does not, and they are wrong. No serious doctor or scientist could have witnessed the remarkable improvement in the health of HIV-infected individuals on modern treatment without acknowledging that truth. The mortality from AIDS in some British hospitals has fallen tenfold since the drugs became available. The drugs work—which is just as well, given their cost.

A Strict Regimen

To begin with they did not work. Initially, each promising drug was met with rapid disappointment as the virus became resistant. And then, in 1995, the penny dropped—some might say a bit belatedly. What was needed was not single drugs, but a combination of at least three.

New drugs have come—and gone—but that is the essence of treatment. With these drugs you can prevent HIV from developing into full-blown AIDS and even bring the desperately ill back from the brink. Sadly, though, it is not that simple. If you do not take the drugs properly, the virus comes back in a resistant form which may be impossible to treat. 'Properly' means that you really need adherence approach-

Friends and family attend a funeral for a South African woman who died of AIDS. Most African nations lack sufficient healthcare funds to contend with the AIDS crisis.

ing 100 per cent to the drug regimen. Treatment—as far as we know—needs to be maintained for a lifetime, because the virus simply comes back if it is stopped.

In Britain HIV units have achieved the best results in the world. Encouraging 100 per cent adherence is a tremendous feat achieved by dedicated and inspired teams of nurses, doctors, health advisers, community specialists, scientists and pharmacists. Patients attend regularly for follow-up in clinics and have a battery of expensive tests performed at every attendance. All drugs have side-effects and these need to be screened for (a major cause of HIV morbidity and mortality is now drug complications), and you have to test for response of, and resistance to, the virus.

Drugs Will Not Work in Africa

It is absurd to suppose that Western medicine will solve the problem in Africa. Even if the drugs were provided free, you would need, by African standards, impossibly expensive support facilities to monitor the effects of treatment. One major London teaching hospital

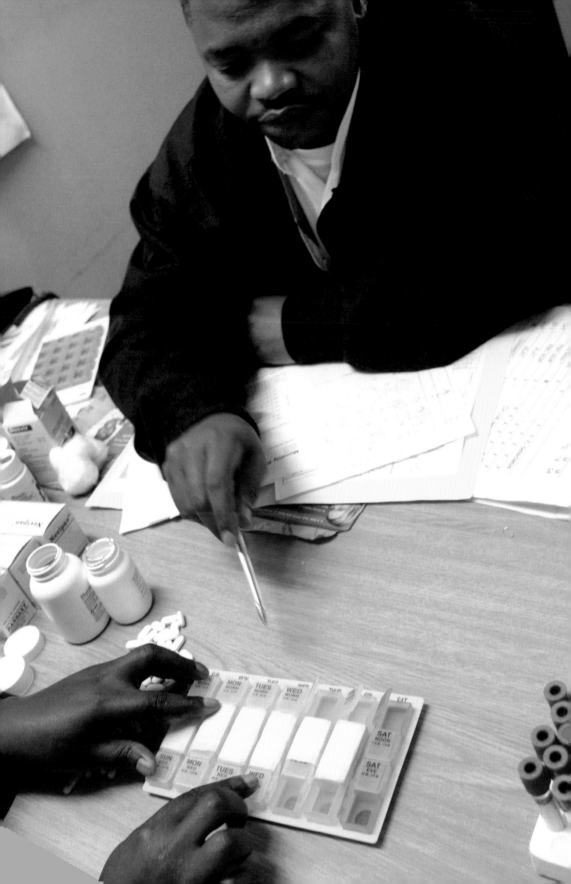

has a budget of about 20 million [pounds sterling] a year to treat 2,000 patients with HIV. This compares with a per capita health-care budget for all medical problems of $20 per person per year in Uganda, which is far from the poorest of African nations.

And that is where the problem lies. Without proper scientific support, just handing out free drugs in Africa will not cure people of HIV. This is my point and, for different reasons, Mbeki's. In Africa, AIDS is not a consequence of HIV but of poverty.

FAST FACT

A 2003 study showed that about 10 percent of the new AIDS cases in Europe are drug-resistant strains.

There is worse. Resistant virus can be transmitted from person to person, and by handing out drugs without proper back-up we would run the risk of a second wave of primarily resistant virus spreading worldwide. This is where the lesson from TB [tuberculosis] is vital. TB is a far easier disease to treat. In Britain we expect cure rates of greater than 90 per cent for the lung form, after usually just six months of treatment. Let us compare that with the situation in, for example, Nigeria. In one study it was established that nearly half of all drugs offered for treatment of TB there were out-of-date, incorrectly prescribed or fake.

Apart from money, you also need a social structure in which to implement your treatment. In a depressingly common development, the Nigerian study had to be abandoned halfway through because of civil unrest. The cure rate for TB in the Third World is, not surprisingly, about 10 per cent. Up to 15 per cent of isolates of TB in those countries show evidence of resistance, and there have already been outbreaks of fatal, multiple-resistant TB in London and New York.

Free Drugs Are Not the Answer

So what can be done in Africa? The answer is, to most HIV clinicians, screamingly obvious. There are already some limited measures

A South African health-care worker instructs an HIV-positive patient on how to take her medications. Patients taking AIDS drugs must follow a very strict regimen.

in practice: routine condom use and public-health messages; treatment of sexually transmitted diseases which enhance HIV transmission; use of cheap, life-saving pneumonia preventers like Septrin; and Caesarean sections for affected mothers.

But what the banners of protesters outside the drug companies ought to be saying is not 'Free Drugs' but 'Where Are Your Vaccines?'. Most vaccines require one or two injections, in contrast to a lifetime's dependence on drugs that are proving highly lucrative for the pharmaceutical industry. The number of scientists working on HIV vaccines throughout the world is about 100. Almost none of them works for commercial drug companies. As they say in America, go figure.

EVALUATING THE AUTHORS' ARGUMENTS:

The author of this viewpoint believes that if Africans were supplied with AIDS drugs, they would not be able to use them effectively. Edward Susman, the author of the previous viewpoint disagrees. He believes that Africans can use these drugs as effectively as people in Western nations. What evidence does each author use to support his argument? Whose argument is more persuasive? Why?

VIEWPOINT 5

Africa Needs Foreign Money to Fight AIDS

George W. Bush

"America has increased total spending to fight AIDS overseas by nearly 100 percent. . . . But we must do far more."

Africa urgently needs large sums of monetary aid in order to fight the devastation being caused by AIDS, maintains George W. Bush in the following viewpoint. According to Bush, the United States has already contributed significant funds to prevention and treatment in Africa, and this has been effective. However, he argues, both the United States and other countries need to contribute much more in order to make a significant impact on this disease. Bush is the former governor of Texas and the forty-third president of the United States.

AS YOU READ, CONSIDER THE FOLLOWING QUESTIONS:
1. How much will the United States contribute to fighting AIDS under the Emergency Plan for AIDS Relief?
2. As explained by the author, what does Uganda prove about AIDS prevention?
3. According to Bush, of the more than 4 million people needing immediate drug treatment in sub-Saharan Africa, what percentage are receiving it?

George W. Bush, "President Urges Congress to Act Quickly on Global HIV/AIDS Initiative," www.whitehouse.gov, April 29, 2003.

HIV/AIDS is a tragedy for millions of men, women and children, and a threat to stability of entire countries and of regions of our world. Our nations have the ability and, therefore, the duty to confront this grave public health crisis. . . .

Africa Needs International Help

Confronting this tragedy is the responsibility of every nation. For the United States, it is a part of the special calling that began with our founding. We believe in the dignity of life, and this conviction determines our conduct around the world. We believe that everyone has a right to liberty, including the people of Afghanistan and Iraq. We believe that everyone has a right to life, including children in the cities and villages of Africa and the Caribbean.

Today [2003], on the continent of Africa alone nearly 30 million people are living with HIV/AIDS, including 3 million people under the age of 15 years old. In Botswana, nearly 40 percent of the adult population—40 percent—has HIV, and projected life expectancy has fallen more than 30 years due to AIDS. In seven sub-Sahara African countries, mortality for children under age five has increased by 20 to 40 percent because of AIDS.

There are only two possible responses to suffering on this scale. We can turn our eyes away in resignation and despair, or we can take decisive, historic action to turn the tide against this disease and give the hope of life to millions who need our help now. The United States of America chooses the path of action and the path of hope.

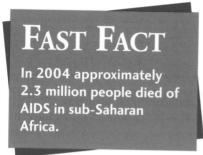

FAST FACT

In 2004 approximately 2.3 million people died of AIDS in sub-Saharan Africa.

Since January 2001, America has increased total spending to fight AIDS overseas by nearly 100 percent. We've already pledged more than $1.6 billion to the global fund to fight AIDS and other infectious diseases. It is by far the most of any nation in the world today. And last year [2002], I launched an initiative to help prevent the transmission of HIV from mothers to children in Africa and the Caribbean.

President Bush meets with schoolchildren in Botswana. According to Bush, the United States contributes significant resources to the global fight against AIDS.

"We Must Do Far More"

These are vital efforts and they're important efforts. But we must do far more. So in January [2003], I asked the House and the Senate to enact the Emergency Plan for AIDS Relief. . . . This plan will direct $15 billion to fight AIDS abroad over the next five years, beginning with $2 billion in 2004. We will create comprehensive systems [to] diagnose, to treat and to prevent AIDS in 14 African and Caribbean countries where the disease is heavily concentrated. We won't diminish our other efforts that are now ongoing. We will continue the funding that is in place, but we'll focus intensely on 14 ravaged countries to show the world what is possible.

This is a terrible disease, but it is not a hopeless disease. At this moment, nations around the world, governments and health officials, doctors and nurses, people living with the virus are proving that there is hope, and that lives can be saved. We know that AIDS can be prevented. In Uganda . . . President [Yoweri] Museveni has begun a comprehensive program in 1986 with a prevention strategy emphasizing abstinence and marital fidelity, as well as condoms, to prevent HIV transmission.

The results are encouraging. The AIDS infection rate in Uganda has fallen dramatically since 1990. And in places throughout the country, the percentage of pregnant women with HIV has been cut in half. Congress should make the Ugandan approach the model for our prevention efforts under the emergency plan.

We also know that AIDS can be treated. Anti-retroviral drugs[1]

President Bush passes beneath an AIDS logo during a visit to a hospital in Nigeria.

have become much more affordable in many nations, and they are extending many lives. In Africa, as more AIDS patients take these drugs, doctors are witnessing what they call the Lazarus effect, when one patient is rescued by medicine, as if back from the dead. Many others with AIDS seek testing and treatment, because it is the first sign of hope they have ever seen.

Many past international efforts to fight AIDS focused on a prevention at the expense of treatment. But people with this disease cannot

1. drugs that delay the onset of AIDS and prolong and improve the quality of life for AIDS patients

be written off as expendable. Integrating care and treatment with prevention is the cornerstone of my emergency plan for AIDS relief, and we know it works. . . .

In Uganda's capital, a clinical research center is providing anti-retroviral therapy to 6,000 patients with HIV. Health care workers from other centers in Uganda travel by truck and by motorcycle to rural villages and farms a few times each week, delivering critical medicine to patients who cannot reach the city for treatment.

These are successful strategies, and must be brought to a much larger scale. . . .

In sub-Sahara Africa, just one percent of the more than 4 million people needing immediate drug treatment are receiving medicine. That's about 50,000 people. The Emergency Plan for AIDS Relief is designed to put major resources behind proven methods of care and treatment

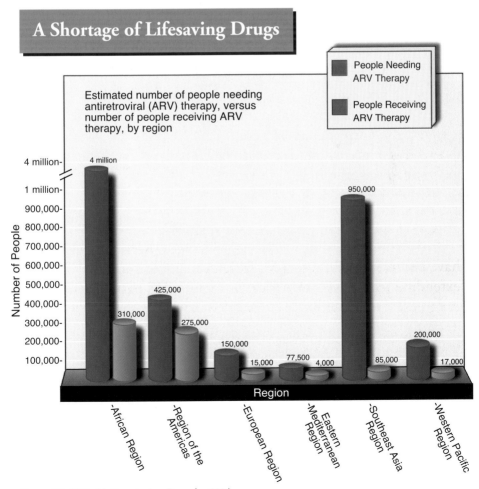

A Shortage of Lifesaving Drugs

Estimated number of people needing antiretroviral (ARV) therapy, versus number of people receiving ARV therapy, by region

People Needing ARV Therapy

People Receiving ARV Therapy

Number of People

Region

African Region: 4 million, 310,000
Region of the Americas: 425,000, 275,000
European Region: 150,000, 15,000
Eastern Mediterranean Region: 77,500, 4,000
Southeast Asia Region: 950,000, 85,000
Western Pacific Region: 200,000, 17,000

Source: World Health Organization, December 2004.

and prevention, and multiply these goods—good works many times over. . . .

Our experts believe that the Emergency Plan for AIDS Relief will, in this decade, prevent 7 million new HIV infections, treat at least 2 million people with life extending drugs, and provide humane care for millions of people suffering from AIDS—and, as importantly— for children orphaned by AIDS.

A Moral Imperative

Confronting the threat of AIDS is important work, and it is urgent work. It is a moral imperative for our great nation. In the three months since I announced the emergency plan, an estimated 760,000 people have died from AIDS, 1.2 million people have been infected, more than 175,000 babies have been born with the virus. Time is not on our side. . . .

Africa, the Caribbean and the United States cannot [succeed] by ourselves. I urge all nations, and will continue to urge all nations, to join with us in this great effort.

Fighting AIDS on a global scale is a massive and complicated undertaking. Yet, this cause is rooted in the simplest of moral duties. When we see this kind of preventable suffering, when we see a plague leaving graves and orphans across a continent, we must act. When we see the wounded traveler on the road to Jericho, we will not, America will not, pass to the other side of the road.

EVALUATING THE AUTHOR'S ARGUMENTS:

In this viewpoint George W. Bush uses persuasive language to support his contention that Africa needs more foreign aid. Give two examples of this type of language. How does it strengthen Bush's argument?

Africa Needs Health Care System Improvements to Fight AIDS

Holly Burkhalter

"The biggest limiting factor for AIDS treatment . . . is the paucity of trained health care workers."

Holly Burkhalter is the U.S. policy director of Physicians for Human Rights and its Health Action AIDS Campaign. In the following viewpoint she maintains that regardless of how much money is donated to fighting AIDS in Africa, progress against the disease will be limited by the shortage of health care workers there. Without a sustainable health care system to care for AIDS patients, AIDS drugs will not prevent AIDS, she argues. In fact, says Burkhalter, foreign aid may be intensifying this problem because many African health care workers leave their jobs for foreign-funded AIDS programs. In her opinion, significant foreign aid must go toward helping Africa improve its health care infrastructure.

Holly Burkhalter, "Misplaced Help in the AIDS Fight," *The Washington Post*, vol. 21, May 31–June 6, 2004. Copyright © 2004 by The Washington Post Book World Service/Washington Post Writers Group. Reproduced by permission of the author.

AS YOU READ, CONSIDER THE FOLLOWING QUESTIONS:
1. As explained by the author, what does Malawi reveal about the effects of foreign donations to fight AIDS?
2. What effect does the donor community often have on health sector personnel and national health care budgets, according to Burkhalter?
3. In the author's opinion, what goals should the United States strive for in addition to treating AIDS?

When it comes to the HIV-AIDS pandemic, generosity isn't enough. Wealthy nations' contributions to fight the disease are unwittingly and unnecessarily exacerbating another crisis in some poor countries: the staggering shortage of health care personnel. African doctors and nurses are leaving public-sector jobs in droves to take more lucrative positions in foreign-funded HIV-AIDS programs. Public hospitals and clinics are being stripped of staffers; rural and slum outposts are being abandoned. The United States, the world's largest donor in the HIV-AIDS crisis, must also take the lead in supporting primary health care infrastructure and nourishing Africa's overwhelmed, underpaid nurses, doctors and other health workers.

Losing Health Care Workers

Malawi, a painfully poor southern African country with upward of 850,000 HIV-infected people, shows what happens when well-meaning but myopic donors fund AIDS-only initiatives. Doctors from the capital's Lilongwe Central Hospital reported recently that it is hemorrhaging personnel from its wards. The 970-bed facility employs only 169 nurses to staff 520 positions. Its six laboratory technicians are doing the work of the 38 once employed there.

Where have all the health care workers gone? Tens of thousands have succumbed to a global "brain drain" and are working in clinics and hospitals in the United States, Britain and Canada. But an increasing number have been hired by nongovernmental organizations or foreign universities that are setting up HIV-AIDS prevention and treatment projects in Africa.

Programs to achieve universal access to AIDS treatment are desperately needed, and they do require trained medical staff. But if resources are drained from poor communities or diverted from other health priorities, deaths from different causes could mount, leaving some communities worse off than before the donors arrived. Compounding the problem, the donor community itself is sometimes directly responsible for bone-deep cuts in health sector personnel and stringent caps on national health care budgets. In AIDS-stricken Kenya, more than 4,000 nurses and several thousand other health workers are unemployed, thanks to macroeconomic constraints championed by the International Monetary Fund and foreign donors.

A woman comforts a sick relative in a hospital in Malawi. The hospital is woefully understaffed to meet its patients' needs.

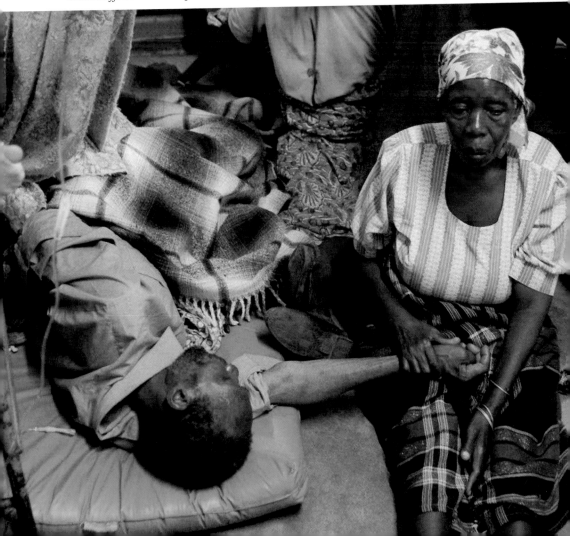

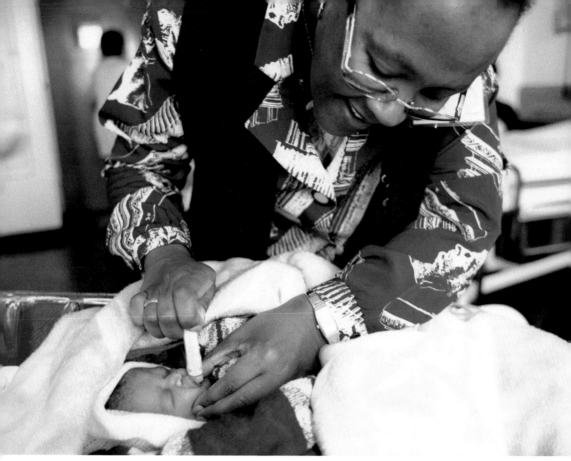

A South African nurse administers a dose of medication to an HIV-positive baby. Many African countries lack enough health care workers to properly care for AIDS patients.

Misplaced Help

President Bush boldly committed to provide AIDS treatment to 2 million people over the next five years[1]—a welcome departure from the previous decade, when the United States did not provide antiretroviral treatment to a single African. But reaching those goals requires much more than buying drugs and training Africans to use them. The fact is, there are not enough local health care workers in Africa to meet even modest treatment goals. Consider Botswana, with a third of a million HIV-positive people. Several years ago the Gates Foundation and other donors provided enough resources to treat everyone in the country. But a crippling shortage of health care workers at every level, among other problems, has limited the rollout of antiretrovirals to only 21,000 of the 110,000 who need them now to stay alive.

1. Under the U.S. Emergency Plan for AIDS Relief, the United States has pledged $15 billion over five years to help fight AIDS worldwide.

It won't be easy, but there is another way. First, U.S. AIDS czar [coordinator of United States Government Activities to Combat HIV/AIDS Globally] Randall Tobias should announce his intention to meet not only ambitious treatment objectives but goals of equity and sustainability. If treatment numbers alone drive AIDS policy, the United States could end up serving those easiest to reach—the urban well-to-do—while the few health services available to the poorest of the poor will be raided and degraded. Embedding AIDS programs into primary health care, adding basic health care to new free-standing treatment initiatives and keeping a scorecard on the distribution of resources among the poorest areas of AIDS-burdened countries would help reverse that trend and provide resources for other health needs as well.

Second, the president should ask Congress for the additional billions of dollars required every year to help build the health care infrastructure needed for both HIV-AIDS treatment programs and overall public health. Some of that money should be given to support the World Health Organization's "3 by 5" initiative, a strategy to provide AIDS treatment to 3 million people by the year 2005.

Because the local hospital lacks the resources to accommodate them, a health care worker in South Africa pays a visit to the home of a woman with AIDS and her HIV-positive son.

Third, Tobias should jettison an outworn axiom of development policy: that foreign donors should not provide remuneration for civil servants, including health care workers, because it inevitably fosters dependency and ultimately is unsustainable. The AIDS pandemic in Africa is in such a death spiral that entire countries have become unsustainable. It is past time for the United States to provide resources not just to American universities, contractors and nongovernmental organizations but to African health workers themselves in the form of health insurance and care, salary enhancements where possible, school fees, and housing allowances. These resources should be targeted to all underpaid nurses, doctors, pharmacists and health workers, not just those providing AIDS services.

Running Out of People

Today the biggest limiting factor for AIDS treatment in the developing world is the paucity of trained health care workers. As one worried U.S. executive branch official said privately, "We're going to run out of people before we run out of money." President Bush and his AIDS team can clear that obstacle by giving more resources directly to African nurses, midwives and doctors, especially those who provide care through fragile public health systems to the people who need it most: the destitute and the marginalized.

EVALUATING THE AUTHORS' ARGUMENTS:

In sub-Saharan Africa, 25.4 million people are infected with HIV. An estimated 3.1 million new infections occurred there in 2004. The authors in Chapter 3 of this book offer various solutions to the problem. If you were to write an essay about the best way to help fight AIDS in Africa, what strategy/strategies would you advocate? Back up your answer with evidence from the viewpoints.

FACTS ABOUT AIDS

Facts About the Virus

- Acquired Immunodeficiency Syndrome (AIDS) results from infection with the Human Immunodeficiency Virus (HIV).
- HIV is transmitted by bodily fluids such as blood, semen, breast milk, and vaginal secretions. HIV is not a hardy organism; the virus dies within about twenty minutes once it is outside a human body.
- HIV causes disease by infecting cells that normally coordinate a person's immune response to infection. When this happens, that person is prone to a range of diseases that a healthy person's body is normally able to fight off.
- Studies suggest that the virus spread initially in West Africa, but it is possible that there were several separate initial sources, corresponding to the different strains of HIV that exist.
- AIDS has claimed 20 million lives worldwide.
- Most people living with HIV are unaware they are infected.
- There is currently no cure or vaccine for HIV or AIDS.

Approximately 39 Million People Around the World Are Estimated to Be Living with HIV/AIDS

- 25.4 million live in sub-Saharan Africa.
- 7.1 million live in South and Southeast Asia.
- 1.7 million live in Latin America.
- 1.4 million live in Eastern Europe and Central Asia.
- 1.1 million live in East Asia.
- 1 million live in North America.

New Infections

- During 2004 an estimated 4.9 million people became newly infected with HIV, including approximately 640,000 children under 15 years old.
- Women comprise a growing percentage of new HIV/AIDS cases; in 2004, approximately 47 percent of people with HIV/AIDS were women.
- Young people, aged 15 to 24, account for approximately half of new adult HIV infections.

- An estimated 15 million children living in 2004 have been orphaned due to AIDS.
- HIV is the leading cause of death worldwide among people aged 15 to 59

AIDS in Africa
- Sub-Saharan Africa has approximately 10 percent of the world's population, but it is home to 64 percent of people living with HIV/AIDS.
- Over 20 percent of adults in sub-Saharan Africa are estimated to be HIV-positive.
- South Africa has the greatest number of people in one country living with HIV/AIDS (5.3 million).
- Swaziland has the highest rate of HIV/AIDS in the world (38.8 percent).
- Many of the nations hardest hit by AIDS also suffer from malnutrition, food insecurity, and famine.

Global Spending to Fight AIDS
- In 2004 global spending on HIV/AIDS was estimated to be $6.1 billion.
- The Joint United Nations Programme on HIV/AIDS projects that for 2005, $12 billion will be needed to effectively respond to the HIV/AIDS epidemic, and that by 2007, this will rise to $20 billion.
- Ninety-five percent of the people living with HIV/AIDS reside in low- and middle-income countries.

Facts About AIDS in the United States
- Approximately 1.5 million people in the United States have been infected with HIV, including more than 500,000 who have already died.
- Minorities represent 71 percent of new AIDS cases and comprise 64 percent of those estimated to be living with HIV.
- African Americans make up 13 percent of the U.S. population, but account for 49 percent of new AIDS diagnoses.
- Latinos account for 20 percent of new AIDS diagnoses.

Important Dates in the History of AIDS
- The earliest case of confirmed HIV was found in blood samples of an African man who died in 1959.

- In 1981 the Centers for Disease Control published the first reports of a devastating new disease that would come to be known around the world as AIDS.
- Scientists named this new disease AIDS in 1982. By this time, fourteen nations had reported AIDS cases.
- In 1983 researchers at the Pasteur Institute in France identified the HIV that causes AIDS. The disease had then been reported in thirty-three countries.
- Azidothymidine (AZT), the first anti-HIV drug, was approved by the U.S. Food and Drug Administration in 1987.
- In 1988 the World Health Organization began World AIDS Day to focus attention on fighting the disease.
- By 1991 10 million people worldwide were estimated to be HIV-positive.
- In 1996 studies showed that triple-drug therapy could effectively control HIV in some people, delaying the onset of AIDS, reducing the symptoms, and extending patients' life spans.

ORGANIZATIONS TO CONTACT

The editors have compiled the following list of organizations concerned with the issues debated in this book. The descriptions are derived from materials provided by the organizations. All have publications or information available for interested readers. The list was compiled on the day of publication of the present volume; names, addresses, phone and fax numbers, and e-mail and Internet addresses may change. Be aware that many organizations take several weeks or longer to respond to inquiries, so allow as much time as possible.

AIDS Vaccine Advocacy Coalition (AVAC)
101 W. Twenty-third St., #2227, New York, NY 10011
(212) 367-1084
e-mail: avac@avac.org
Web site: www.avac.org

AVAC is a community- and consumer-based organization founded in 1995 to accelerate the ethical development and global delivery of vaccines for HIV/AIDS. The organization provides independent analysis, policy advocacy, public education, and mobilization to enhance AIDS research. It also provides the AVAC Update Newsbook, "Community Perspective in Research, Advocacy, and Progress."

Alive and Well AIDS Alternatives
111684 Ventura Blvd., #338, Studio City, CA 91604
(877) 411-AIDS
fax: (818) 780-7093
e-mail: info@aliveandwell.org
Web site: www.aliveandwell.org

Alive and Well AIDS Alternatives challenges popular beliefs and theories about HIV and AIDS. It sponsors clinical studies and scientific research in an attempt to verify the central tenets about the disease, its cause, and its treatments. The organization also publishes the book *What If Everything You Thought You Knew About AIDS Was Wrong?*

American Foundation for AIDS Research (AmFAR)
733 Third Ave., 12th Fl., New York, NY 10097
(212) 682-7440
fax: (212) 682-9812
Web site: www.amfar.org

The American Foundation for AIDS Research supports AIDS prevention and research and advocates AIDS-related public policy. It publishes several monographs, compendiums, journals, and periodic publications, including the *AIDS/HIV Treatment Directory,* published twice a year, the newsletter *HIV/AIDS Educator and Reporter,* published three times every year, and the quarterly *AmFAR Newsletter.*

American Red Cross AIDS Education Office
1709 New York Ave. NW, Suite 208, Washington, DC 20006
(202) 434-4074
e-mail: info@usa.redcross.org
Web site: www.redcross.org

Established in 1881, the American Red Cross is one of America's oldest public health organizations. Its AIDS Education Office publishes pamphlets, brochures, and posters containing facts about AIDS. These materials are available at local Red Cross chapters. In addition, many chapters offer informational videotapes, conduct presentations, and operate speakers bureaus.

The Beyond Awareness Campaign
+27 11 880-8868
e-mail: actpso@effectcompany.org
Web site: www.aidsinfo.co.za

The Beyond Awareness Campaign is a project of the HIV/AIDS and STD (sexually transmitted diseases) Directorate of the South African Department of Health. The site details a wide range of communications activities undertaken as part of a national campaign. Many useful documents that are relevant in Africa and internationally can be downloaded.

Center for Women Policy Studies (CWPS)
1221 Connecticut Ave. NW, Suite 312, Washington, DC 20036
(202) 872-1770
fax: (202) 296-8962
e-mail: cwps@centerwomenpolicy.org
Web site: www.centerwomenpolicy.org

The CWPS was the first national policy institute to focus specifically on issues affecting the social, legal, and economic status of women. It believes that the government and the medical community have neglected the effect of AIDS on women and that more action should be taken to help women who have AIDS. The center publishes the book *The Guide to Resources on Women and AIDS* and produces the video *Fighting for Our Lives: Women Confronting AIDS.*

Centers for Disease Control and Prevention (CDC)
National AIDS Clearinghouse, PO Box 6003
Rockville, MD 20849-6003
(800) 458-5231
fax: (301) 738-6616
e-mail: aidsinfo@cdcnac.org
Web site: www.cdcnac.org

The CDC is the government agency charged with protecting the public health by preventing and controlling diseases and by responding to public health emergencies. The CDC National AIDS Clearinghouse is a reference, referral, and distribution service for HIV/AIDS-related information. All of the clearinghouse's services are designed to facilitate the sharing of information and resources among people working in HIV/AIDS prevention, treatment, and support services. The CDC publishes information about the disease in the *HIV/AIDS Prevention Newsletter* and the *Morbidity and Mortality Weekly Report.*

Family Research Council
700 Thirteenth St. NW, Suite 500, Washington, DC 20005
(202) 393-2100
fax: (202) 393-2134
e-mail: corrdept@frc.org
Web site: www.frc.org

The Family Research Council promotes the traditional family unit and the Judeo-Christian value system. The council opposes the public education system's tolerance of homosexuality and condom distribution programs, which its members believe encourage sexual promiscuity and lead to the spread of AIDS. It publishes numerous reports from a conservative perspective, including the monthly newsletter *Washington Watch* and the bimonthly journal *Family Policy*.

Global AIDS Interfaith Alliance (GAIA)
The Presidio of San Francisco, PO Box 29110
San Francisco, CA 94129-0110
(415) 461-7196
fax: (415) 461-9681
e-mail: info@thegaia.org
Web site: www.thegaia.org

GAIA is a nonprofit organization composed of top AIDS researchers and doctors, religious leaders, and African medical officials, most of whom are associated with religiously based clinics and hospitals. The organization is concerned with infrastructure development and the training of prevention educators and personnel to conduct HIV testing and counseling. It also emphasizes the modification of values, structures, and practices that predispose women and girls to higher HIV infection rates than men, that stigmatize ill persons, and that contribute to public denial. GAIA's Web site offers news and updates about AIDS.

Health, Education, AIDS Liaison (HEAL)
(416) 406-HEAL
e-mail: inquiries@healtoronto.com
Web site: www.healtoronto.com

HEAL is a network of international chapters that challenges the validity of the traditional HIV/AIDS hypothesis and the efficacy of HIV drug treatments. HEAL believes that debate and open inquiry are fundamental parts of the scientific process and should not be abandoned to accommodate the theory of HIV. Its Web site provides articles that question the link between HIV and AIDS and offers information about HIV tests, AIDS in Africa, and drug treatments.

International AIDS Vaccine Initiative (IAVI)
110 William St., New York, NY 10038
(212) 847-1111
fax: (212) 847-1112
e-mail: info@iavi.org
Web site: www.iavi.org

IAVI is a global organization working to speed the development and distribution of preventative AIDS vaccines. IAVI's work focuses on mobilizing support through advocacy and education, acceleration of scientific progress, encouraging industrial participation in AIDS vaccine development, and assuring global access to the vaccines once they are developed. IAVI publishes fact sheets and policy papers about its programs and a variety of issues concerning AIDS vaccine development.

International Council of AIDS Services Organizations (ICASO)
399 Church St., 4th Fl., Toronto, ON M5B ZJ6, Canada
(416) 340-2437
fax: (416) 340-8224
Web site: www.icaso.org

ICASO is a network of community-based AIDS organizations that brings together groups throughout the world that have arisen out of community efforts to control the spread and impact of HIV/AIDS. It recognizes human rights as being central to an intelligent public health strategy to combat the epidemic. The ICASO network is an interactive global focus point in the international HIV/AIDS world, gathering and disseminating information and analysis on key issues. ICASO provides news and information about AIDS, including *HIV/AIDS and Human Rights— Stories from the Frontlines.*

Joint United Nations Programme on HIV/AIDS (UNAIDS)
20 Ave. Appia, CH-1211, Geneva 27, Switzerland
(4122) 791-3666
fax: (4122) 791-4187
e-mail: unaids@unaids.org
Web site: www.unaids.org

UNAIDS is a joint United Nations program on HIV/AIDS created by the combination of six organizations. It is a leading advocate for worldwide action against HIV/AIDS, and its global mission is to lead, strengthen, and support an expanded response to the AIDS epidemic that will prevent the spread of HIV, provide care and support for those infected and affected by HIV/AIDS, and alleviate the socioeconomic and human impact of the epidemic. UNAIDS has many publications, including *HIV/AIDS Human Resources and Sustainable Development,* and *Young People and HIV/AIDS: Opportunity in Crisis.*

National AIDS Fund
1030 Fifteenth St. NW, Suite 860, Washington, DC 20005
(202) 408-4848
fax: (202) 408-1818
e-mail: info@aidsfund.org
Web site: www.aidsfund.org

The National AIDS Fund seeks to eliminate HIV as a major health and social problem. Its members work in partnership with the public and private sectors to provide care and to prevent new infections in communities and in the workplace by means of advocacy, grants, research, and education. The fund publishes the monthly newsletter, *News from the National AIDS Fund,* which is also available through its Web site.

National Association of People with AIDS (NAPWA)
1413 K St. NW, Washington, DC 20005-3442
(202) 898-0414
fax: (202) 898-0435
e-mail: napwa@thecure.org
Web site: www.thecure.org

NAPWA is an organization that represents people with HIV. Its members believe that it is the inalienable right of every person with HIV to have health care, to be free from discrimination, to have the right to a dignified death, to be adequately housed, to be protected from violence, and to travel and immigrate regardless of country of origin or HIV status. The association publishes several informational materials such as an annual strategic agenda and the annual *Community Report.*

Rockford Institute
934 N. Main St., Rockford, IL 61103
(815) 964-5053
e-mail: rkfdinst@bossnt.com

The Rockford Institute seeks to rebuild moral values and recover the traditional American family. It believes that AIDS is a symptom of the decline of the traditional family, and it insists that only by supporting traditional families and moral behavior will America rid itself of the disease. The institute publishes the periodicals *Family in America* and the *Religion & Society Report* as well as various syndicated newspaper articles that occasionally deal with the topic of AIDS.

FOR FURTHER READING

Books

Tony Barnett and Alan Whiteside, *AIDS in the Twenty-First Century: Disease and Globalization.* New York: Palgrave Macmillan, 2003. The authors—experts in their field for fifteen years—examine the social and economic effects of the HIV/AIDS epidemic, failures in responding to it, and what must be done to combat the epidemic.

Greg Behrman, *The Invisible People: How the U.S. Has Slept Through the Global AIDS Pandemic, the Greatest Humanitarian Catastrophe of Our Time.* New York: Free Press, 2004. Examines the U.S. response to the global AIDS crisis and how this disease is reshaping the social, economic, and political dimensions of the world.

Catherine Campbell, *Letting Them Die: Why HIV/AIDS Prevention Programmes Fail.* Bloomington: Indiana University Press, 2003. Examines why people in AIDS-ravaged countries continue to engage in unsafe sex and why programs designed to prevent this practice often fail.

Michelle Cochrane, *When AIDS Began: San Francisco and the Making of an Epidemic.* New York: Routledge, 2004. Through her examination of the early outbreaks of AIDS in San Francisco, the author offers insight into how this disease spreads.

Larry O. Gostin, *The AIDS Pandemic: Complacency, Injustice, and Unfulfilled Expectations.* Chapel Hill: University of North Carolina, 2004. A collection of essays that discuss the controversial issues surrounding AIDS, and the way the disease impacts both the infected and the uninfected.

Edward C. Green, *Rethinking AIDS Prevention: Learning from Successes in Developing Countries.* Westport, CT: Praeger, 2003. The author, a member of the President's Advisory Committee on HIV/AIDS, examines how and why some countries have succeeded in reducing HIV infection rates.

Emma Guest, *Children of AIDS: Africa's Orphan Crisis.* London: Sterling, 2003. Based on extensive interviews, this book reveals how AIDS has created millions of orphans in Africa and how this will affect that country and the rest of the world.

Susan Hunter, *Black Death: AIDS in Africa.* New York: Palgrave Macmillan, 2003. Examines the history of AIDS in Africa and the extent of the disease there.

Alexander Irwin, *Global AIDS: Myths and Facts; Tools for Fighting the AIDS Pandemic.* Cambridge, MA: South End Press, 2003. Discusses common myths about the treatment and prevention of HIV and AIDS and how these myths affect the spread of the disease worldwide.

Jacob Levenson, *The Secret Epidemic: The Story of AIDS and Black America.* New York: Pantheon, 2004. Summarizes recent research on AIDS among African Americans, explaining how AIDS has become a leading cause of death for this group.

Donald E. Messere, *Breaking the Conspiracy of Silence: Christian Churches and the Global AIDS Crisis.* Minneapolis, MN: Augsburg Fortress, 2004. An overview of the historical and future roles of the church in the AIDS crisis.

Raymond A. Smith, *Encyclopedia of AIDS: A Social, Political, Cultural, and Scientific Record of the HIV Epidemic.* New York: Penguin, 2001. Provides a comprehensive look at AIDS and its effects on society, politics, law, and humans, and contains more than three hundred entries contributed by 175 authorities, ranging from academics to doctors.

Shereen Usdin, *The No-Nonsense Guide to HIV/AIDS.* New York: Verso, 2003. Summarizes the origins of the disease, the way it spreads, the profits made by drug companies, and the special vulnerability of women.

Periodicals

Ben Barber, "Successes Against AIDS in Africa," *World & I,* June 2002.

Greg Behrman, "AIDS Fight Demands Serious Money and Serious Plan," *Los Angeles Times,* March 1, 2004.

Laura Berman, "Sex-Abstinence Programs Don't Work," *Chicago Sun-Times,* October 4, 2004.

Patrick Bond, "A Decade of Deadly Denial," *Against the Current,* July/August 2004.

Bono, "Mr. President, Africa Needs Us," *Liberal Opinion Week,* February 10, 2003.

Salih Booker, "To Help Africa Battle AIDS, Write Off Its Debt," *Liberal Opinion Week,* June 3, 2002.

Susan Brink, "AIDS: Darkening in America," *U.S. News & World Report,* July 12, 2004.

Christianity Today, "As Complicated as ABC: Condoms and Abstinence Can Both Play a Role in AIDS Prevention," February 2004.

Economist, "The New Face of AIDS; Women and HIV," November 27, 2004.

Maggie Farley, "Development Curbed by AIDS, U.N. Says," *Los Angeles Times,* July 16, 2004.

Matt Higgins, "Meeting the Afflicted," *Toward Freedom,* Fall 2004.

William Jasper, "Global AIDS Con Game," *New American,* June 2, 2003.

Gary Karch, "Where Have All the AIDS Drugs Gone?" *Z Magazine,* September 2004.

Nicholas D. Kristof, "No Time to Get Squeamish," *New York Times,* May 9, 2003.

Stephen Lewis, "AIDS Has a Woman's Face," *Ms.,* Fall 2004.

Richard Lowry, "A Culture War over Condoms," *Conservative Chronicle,* January 22, 2003.

Richard Morin, "'The Dying Is Just Beginning': South Africa's Government Reacts Slowly as AIDS Claims Much of a Generation," *Washington Post National Weekly Edition,* April 12–18, 2004.

James P. Pinkerton, "As the AIDS Bureaucracy Cashes In, the Prospect of a Cure Dims," *Los Angeles Times,* August 6, 2004.

Hugh Russell, "It's Worse than You Imagined," *Spectator,* March 1, 2003.

Michael Specter, "The Vaccine," *New Yorker,* February 3, 2003.

Brent Staples, "Avoiding the Truth of What's Needed to Fight AIDS: Needle Programs," *New York Times,* July 20, 2004.

Edward Susman, "The Global Face of AIDS," *World & I,* March 2004.

Toronto Star, "Africa's AIDS Pandemic," January 2, 2005.

Kai Wright, "AIDS: Hiding in Plain Sight: How Lurid Reports Obscure the Bigger Story," *Columbia Journalism Review,* March/April 2004.

G. Pascal Zachary, "Shunned by Society," *In These Times,* June 24, 2002.

Web Resources

AIDS Channel.org (www.aidschannel.org). Brings together information and resources from civil society organizations, government and research institutions, media, and others working in the field.

AIDS Education Global Information System (www.aegis.org). A grassroots effort to accumulate information and knowledge about AIDS, this site offers fact sheets, publications, a law library, reference materials, and links.

AIDSnews.org (www.aidsnews.org). This Web site provides lists of useful Internet links and resources as well as AIDS databases.

AIDSonline (www.aidsonline.com). Provides information on AIDS as well as resources and links to other AIDS sites.

AIDS.org (www.aids.org). Features AIDS fact sheets, an AIDS bookstore with online reviews of books about HIV and AIDS, and daily news about AIDS.

The Body (www.thebody.com). This site has information on more than 550 topics, including AIDS basics, a "visual aids" gallery, treatment information, policy and activism, and an "ask the experts" section.

British HIV Association and National AIDS Manual (www.aidsmap.com). Offers basic information on HIV and AIDS, HIV/AIDS statistics, new drugs available, and an extensive listing on international HIV/AIDS service agencies.

National Pediatric and Family HIV Resources Center (www.pedhivaids.org). Offers AIDS news and events, educational material, links to AIDS-related sites, questions and answers, and global AIDS information.

Nigeria-AIDS.org (www.nigeria-aids.org). An information source on HIV/AIDS in Nigeria and West Africa.

Virus Myth (www.virusmyth.net). This Web site contains nearly one thousand articles that claim HIV is harmless, that AIDS is caused by toxic chemicals and drugs, and that HIV tests are worthless.

INDEX

Caribbean, AIDS in, 16–17
Centers for Disease Control and
    Prevention (CDC), 47
    on condom effectiveness, 48,
        89
    on teen sexuality, 46
Chin, James, 24
China, health care spending in,
    72
clinical trials, phases of, 84
condoms
    access to, is vital, 91–92
        con, 94–96, 98
    effectiveness of, 48, 89
    failure rates for, 46
    prevalence in use of, 46
    restrictions on access to,
        88–91
Côte d'Ivoire, 30
Cowley, Geoffrey, 12

deaths, from AIDS
    in Africa, 94
    in United States, 81
    worldwide, 58, 61, 82
Department of Health and
    Human Services, U.S.
    (HHS), 78
developing nations
    tuberculosis cure rate in, 111
    unavailability of antiretroviral
        drugs in, 11–13
Duesberg, Alan, 108
Dylan, Bob, 67

education
    in Africa, impact of AIDS on,
        32

see also sex education
Epimodel (computer simulator),
    38, 40
Europe
    AIDS in, 17–19
    drug-resistant AIDS cases in,
        111

Fumento, Michael, 21

gays/bisexuals, rise of new HIV
    diagnoses in, 19
Gere, Richard, 26–27
Global Fund to Fight AIDS,
    Tuberculosis, and Malaria,
    67, 100
Gloyd, Stephen, 62
Gramckow, Jerry, 45, 96
Green, Edward C., 97, 98

Hammer, Scott, 18
Henry J. Kaiser Family
    Foundation, 25
Hickson, Michael, 11
HIV/AIDS
    in Africa, 11–12, 15
    in Asia, 15–16
    in Caribbean/Latin America,
        16–17
    as chronic illness, 9–11
    efforts to control, should
        focus on
        alleviating poverty, 70–72
        development of health care
            infrastructure, 122–24
        the promiscuous, 76–77
        vaccine development,
            79–80, 112

should focus on the promiscuous, 76–77

Richards, Rodney, 42

Satcher, David, 53
Schulz, Nick, 12
sex education
abstinence-only
as challenge to HIV prevention efforts, 53–54
is effective in combating HIV/AIDS, 46–48
con, 50–52
prevalence of, 54
comprehensive, 50, 54
types of, youth sexual activity and, 53
sexually transmitted diseases (STDs), condoms are ineffective in preventing, 47–48
con, 89
Shernoff, Michael, 11
South Africa
growth rate in, effects of HIV/AIDS on, 33
HIV infection in, 30
Spectator (magazine), 37
surveys
on mother-adolescent communication, 52
on teens' perception of AIDS risk, 52
Susman, Edward, 14, 99

Thailand, reduction of HIV/AIDS in, 76
Timaeus, Ian, 40

Tobias, Randall L., 55, 123, 124
tuberculosis, cure rate for, in developing nations, 111

Uganda
antiretroviral drug availability in, 117
decline in HIV infection in, 42, 96–98
UNAIDS. *See* Joint United Nations Programme on HIV/AIDS
United Nations Population Fund (UNFPA), 88
United States
AIDS policy of, 56–58
should focus on expanding health care infrastructure, 123
spending on, 114–15
HIV/AIDS in, 19–20, 126
among African Americans, 70–71
as leading cause of death, 81
new cases of
among gays/bisexuals, 19
in under 25 age group, 50
among women, 71

vaccines, HIV
efforts to control HIV should focus on development of, 79–80
preventive vs. therapeutic, 82–83
spending on, 56
testing of, 80–81, 83–84
would be more effective than drugs in Africa, 112

van de Vijer, David, 18, 19
virginity pledges, use of protection and, 50

Wiessing, Lucas, 18
Winn, Pete, 93
women
    Bush administration efforts against exploitation of, 57–58
    as proportion of adults living with AIDS, 18

youth
    new HIV infection among, 126
    in United States, 50
    sexual activity among, 46, 50
    sex education and, 53
Youth Risk Behavior Survey (CDC, 2001), 46

Zambia, effects of HIV/AIDS on education in, 33

PICTURE CREDITS

ABOUT THE EDITOR

Andrea C. Nakaya, a native New Zealander, holds a BA in English and an MA in communication from San Diego State University. She has spent more than three years at Greenhaven Press, where she works as a full-time book editor. Andrea currently lives in Encinitas, California, with her husband Jamie. In her free time she enjoys traveling, reading, gardening, waterskiing, and snowboarding.